'Thank you for——' She faltered, giving him his cue to leave.

But he was shouldering his way in, already pushing the door shut behind him, and was moving into the room after her as she hastily retreated, reaching out to take her into his arms. She was conscious of his hands coming round her waist, pulling her against him and effectively stopping her escape.

'Mark—I don't——'

'Emma, you do. You want me. . .' His lips softly plundered her own, moving rapidly over her face and mouth and into her hair then back once more to the lips he was tasting like a gourmet. 'Have you worked out my sun sign yet, Emma?' he murmured as he teased her to a helpless response. 'It guarantees we're going to be dynamite together; all the signs say so. . . Come, let me undress you slowly. I want you to remember and relish every moment of this. . .'

WE HOPE you're enjoying our new addition to our Contemporary Romance series—stories which take a light-hearted look at the Zodiac and show that love can be written in the stars!

Every month you can get to know a different combination of star-crossed lovers, with one story that follows the fortunes of a hero or heroine when they embark on the romance of a lifetime with someone born under another sign of the Zodiac. This month features a sizzling love-affair between **Cancer** and **Scorpio**.

To find out more fascinating facts about this month's featured star sign, turn to the back pages of this book. . .

ABOUT THIS MONTH'S AUTHOR

Sally Heywood says: 'I'm a Gemini and I feel we get a really bad press! Just because we like to float around a little bit, then retreat to our special lonely place where we can think things over, other people see us as unreliable, superficial, fickle, cold. . . How can we help it if Gemini's ruler is Mercury, messenger of the gods, and we spend our whole time in mid-flight between heaven and earth?

'Our biggest problem comes when it's time to find the perfect partner; what those born under other signs forget is that along every road there's always another turning and we Geminis long to travel on, out, as far as we can, to the heaven which we know is waiting up ahead. If love is perfect now, then it stands to reason there must be an even more perfect love just beyond our grasp— what could be more romantic?

DARK PASSION

BY

SALLY HEYWOOD

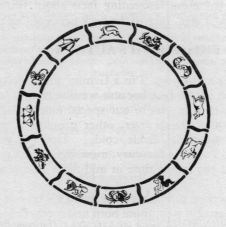

MILLS & BOON LIMITED
ETON HOUSE   18–24 PARADISE ROAD
RICHMOND   SURREY   TW9 1SR

First published in Great Britain 1991
by Mills & Boon Limited

© Sally Heywood 1991

Australian copyright 1991
Philippine copyright 1991
This edition 1991

ISBN 0 263 77133 4

STARSIGN ROMANCES is a trademark of Harlequin Enterprises
B.V., Fribourg Branch. Mills and Boon is an authorised user.

Set in 10 on 11½ pt Linotron Plantin
01-9106-57533z
Typeset in Great Britain by Centracet, Cambridge
Made and printed in Great Britain

CHAPTER ONE

EMMA flicked a duster over the porcelain arrayed on the glass shelf, being careful not to disturb the fragile goods on display, then gently edged her way out of the shop window between a gilt mirror and a shaky credenza which she had lost all hope of selling. Her floral skirt snagged on a corner of the mirror propped against the wall as she squeezed by and she paused, reaching down with one hand to tug at the hem. At that moment she heard the jangle of the old-fashioned shop bell as a customer came in, and by the time she had unhooked her skirt she was conscious that they had walked straight over to her, instead of browsing among the antiques as customers usually did. She lifted her head, but her ready smile froze on her lips. Not a syllable of either surprise or anger escaped her. Slowly she straightened up to her full height of five feet four. One hand feathered through the wisps of dark hair escaping from her upswept hairstyle, and she had the distinct sensation that every nerve in her body was sending out alarm signals.

'So it is you!' grated a voice before she could say anything. It expressed a surprise equal to her own. 'I know you, don't I?' the man went on. 'You were the one making all that fuss at the planning meeting last night. I wondered what your interest was. Now I know.'

Storm-grey eyes roamed briefly round the shop, then turned to subject her also to a similar appraisal. She felt fixed by a brilliant, all-seeing glance, and heard him add, 'This promises to be a very interesting situation.' The voice that offered what she immediately understood as a threat was deep, almost husky. It lacked even the faintest trace of emotion.

A man of around thirty-something, tall, vibrantly fit, he was so handsome, and knew it, that Emma felt herself go on to the defensive at once. She gave him a cold glance. Who did he think he was? His looks were something she hadn't failed to register at the meeting last night. But they didn't give him *carte blanche* to come crashing into her shop as if he owned it, did they? At close quarters, however, she could only re-register first impressions. But that wasn't all she'd noticed then, either. His wealth, his physique, his looks were nothing compared to his aura of dynamic energy. He had so much vitality, he seemed to emit sparks. A go-getter, she judged with disapproval, out to reorganise everybody and everything to suit himself. Well, not me—not me.

He was giving her a thoroughgoing appraisal that left nothing out. She felt taped and docketed. Her resentment flared more fiercely at the thought. But what his final verdict was, she couldn't tell, because he was careful to allow nothing in his face to yield a clue. The enigmatic type. But two could play at that game.

She supposed she must have upset him more than a little last night. Despite his masked expression, the faint aura of aggression in his manner now suggested he wasn't pleased. Skirt free at last, Emma felt it swirl softly round her calves as she moved forward to meet him. Even in her high heels she was still a good head shorter than he was, and she felt a shudder of fright at the prospect of taking on such a man in an all-out battle. But that was how it would have to be.

Everything she possessed was at stake.

But she was puzzled by his words. 'What do you mean, now you know?' she demanded without preamble.

'Now I know the reason for your outrageous verbal

attack on my company last night at the meeting in the town hall.' His face was a blank.

'Oh, that. . .please don't take it personally.' She smiled as sweetly as she could, managing to pull herself together as the shock of meeting him began to wear off. 'I was certainly at the planning meeting. But I wasn't aware I was saying anything outrageous. I simply stated the case as it is. I'm on the defence committee,' she explained without flinching beneath the penetrating gaze he was giving her. 'That's why I was asked to speak.' She paused and added, 'I can't say I noticed you there.'

It was a downright lie. But he hadn't spoken last night, he had merely been ushered in by the city planning officer and then skulked at the back of the hall, taking everything in with empty grey eyes, and walking out at the head of a posse of men just as the meeting came to a noisy close. Remembering his self-confident air, she felt her own ebb once more. 'You won't win,' she forced herself to add, 'so you may as well give in now. We're all against you.'

'I haven't come here to argue with you.' He put a hand to an inside pocket of his steel-grey suit and drew forth a card. 'I want you to come and see me. We need to talk things over. If I'd known who Emma Shields was. . .well, that doesn't matter now. I'm in town for the next five days——'

'Oh, really?' Emma felt her hackles rise. The way his glance silvered over her face, giving her another searching look, made her strongly aware of the power he had over her future, and for an instant she was swept by a feeling of hopelessness at the thought of trying to get the better of such a man. Then her courage asserted itself. She would fight. She had to.

She allowed her glance to travel over his face with the same kind of insolent slowness with which he had

regarded her, trailing over the broad chest, the flat
stomach, over the unending length of him, then back
again, as coolly as he had appraised her, until she
returned to his face and their glances meshed once more.
He was watching her watching him, his face like marble.

Then she forced her glance away and took in the shop
stuffed with the antiques she had acquired over the last
five years. Polished wood, the gleam of veneer and gold,
the sheen of old mirrors and rose velvets and brocades
met her gaze, with, over all, the pervasive scent of
lavender. Emma's spine straightened. She had achieved
something. It was not for this tall, arrogant stranger to
come barging in, trying to belittle it. But when she
eventually forced herself to look at him he returned her
glance with an expression that made her shiver. He had
her number, it said.

Stung, she said quickly, 'Weighing up the strength of
the opposition, Mr—er—er——' Then she peered at
the card he'd pushed into her hand as if she'd already
forgotten it since the previous night. As if everybody in
town didn't know it! It had heralded upheaval, specu-
lation and rumour only adding to its aura of importance.
She'd thought of it as the name of a robber baron—the
man who was going to take all she had. It was all she
could do not to tear his card into little bits and toss them
in his face.

'The name,' he broke in roughly as if he could tell
what was in her mind, 'is Mark del Sarto. And you're
Emma Shields.'

She didn't answer. Why should she give anything
away to a man like this?

'You lease this little place——' he went on.

'So?' Her glance would have withered a lesser mortal.

'You lease it from me now.' He gave a thin smile.
'And you fondly imagine you can dictate what I do with

my own property?' He laughed softly. 'Dream on, Miss Shields. I do what I want, when I want. Get that straight.'

'Is that so?' She arched her brows at him. Her face was flushing with anger already, but she held it in check and gave him a cold stare as if he were something particularly nasty in the woodwork.

'That is very definitely so,' he replied heavily. 'So you'll come and talk things over?' He raised his own dark brows.

'I would have thought,' she said as icily as she could, 'that if you knew so much about me and my views you'd realise it's hardly worth talking. You heard what I said at the meeting last night.'

'So you knew I was there?'

She felt her glance slope away from his. It was as telling as words. To her astonishment he shot out a hand and gripped her by the elbow.

'Stop playing games, Miss Shields. We're going to do business, you and I, whether you like it or not. Understand?'

'Oh, we are?' She felt her flesh burn where he touched it and ripped herself free with more force than was strictly necessary. It made her stumble and she felt a shelf dig into her back. 'Perhaps as a complete stranger you'd like to tell me a few more things about myself?' she enquired in a voice like broken ice. It was meant as a gibe at his cocksure manner, but to her astonishment he began to laugh pleasantly. It lit up his whole face.

'You have an eye for beauty,' he began, letting his eyes skim the many striking *objects d'art* cramming the shop; 'you're intensely feminine, though something of an ice maiden on the surface. On the negative side, you're rather touchy, emotional, apt to fly off the handle when you think you're being pressured——'

'You think you're a bit of an astrologer, do you? Maybe you'd like to tell me my birth sign while you're at it. We may as well have the full picture!' Her lips compressed into a grim line.

'I'll come to that later,' he went on. 'I haven't mentioned your plus side.' He was still smiling and still talking in that flagrantly intimate tone that was making her itch to slap his face. 'You're a wonderful home-maker, wife and mother; you manage to create beauty wherever you go with the most unpromising materials; you love flowers, and sunsets and moonlight—and you're a wonderful lover. . .'

She was speechless. All she wanted was to let fly with a stream of outrage. She found the words on the tip of her tongue—but they stayed there and died. Did he think she was stupid enough to fall for this? It was obvious why he was trying it on. She was the obstacle to his horrible intention to pull down the block. Was she expected not to notice that he'd adroitly brushed aside her objections to his schemes just now? He must think she was stupid as well as all those other things!

She matched his look with a penetrating glance of her own, maintaining eye-contact with a stubbornness that hid the wild racketing of her heartbeats when he didn't drop his glance. This is anger, she registered, amazed at the power-punch of adrenalin he could arouse. It must be because he was trespassing, in her shop, on her territory. Making sure she was aware who really owned it all. The very thought made her want to run into the back room and bolt the door against him. She felt her palms moisten as she forced herself to stand her ground.

He seemed to tick off the signs of emotion chasing over her face, but his own expression remained neutral, eyes empty of any response at all so that she couldn't tell what he was going to say next. When he did speak it was to say simply, 'I wonder if they're compatible.'

'What?' A frown flitted across her brow.

'Our signs,' he replied levelly. There was a faraway look on his face for a moment, but it quickly vanished. Pulling himself together, he went on, 'I'm sure you think yourself far too practical to believe in all that stuff——' he paused '—but perhaps you have a sweet, secret self that hasn't had a chance to come into the open?'

The brisk manner with which he had entered the shop was gone now and he seemed to relax, almost as if he intended to stand and chat, the way her usual customers did, except that none of them would say such outrageously personal things and look at her in this. . .well, this suggestive manner. She prayed for someone to come in and rescue her, but the street door remained firmly shut.

'I'm busy all this week,' she said hurriedly to hide her confusion. 'I couldn't possibly come to see you within the next five days.' Her heart was still doing strange, angry things, and she jerked towards him as if to shepherd him to the door. But he didn't take the cue. They swayed, almost touching for a moment, until she said, 'Please,' before she could stop herself, then, more briskly, 'Would you mind leaving?'

'Leaving?' His lips moved round the word as if he'd never heard it before. 'You can't be trying to tell me you're too busy.'

'I am, actually.'

'Customers queuing at the door!' He laughed, revealing even white teeth and a sudden humorous glint in the grey depths that showed another side of him entirely. Emma wished she hadn't glimpsed it. There was something intriguing about a man who could one minute be arrogant and aggressive, and the next as enchanting as a small boy. But a moment later he switched again and a look of reserve came over him. 'I want to talk business. You'll make time for me if you care about this place of yours. Time's running out. I can be very reasonable. But I'm not going to be kept dangling on a string for long. You'll have to make a decision one way or the other. It's up to you.'

'Decision?' Emma was puzzled. 'I thought it was all decided. By you, that is. You've bought the block and intend to knock it down and build some hideous modern thing here, and we shopkeepers have to get out. End of story.'

'Not end of story, Miss Shields. Not if you talk.'

'I don't see the point of talking. Why should I waste my time doing that when the only purpose would be to salve your conscience?'

'Believe me, my conscience needs nothing of the kind. It's quite clear.'

Emma recoiled from the sharpness in his tone. All she wanted was for him to leave. But she forced herself to say, 'I'm glad you're happy with what you're doing. Most people would feel a slight twinge of guilt at the thought that they were going to cheat six people out of their livelihoods, that they were going to destroy a beautiful old building that has stood on this site for generations, and that they were doing it all for personal gain——'

'I fail to see anything wrong with personal gain,' he cut in.

Emma bit her lip. 'I'll concede, you have to make money in order to live, but the rest stands. This building is one of the nicest ones in the area. There is no forgiving anyone who wants to destroy it.'

'It's falling down!' he began again.

'Nothing that a sensitive landlord couldn't rectify——'

'This is all nonsense,' he broke in firmly. 'And as for doing you out of your livelihood—that's ridiculous. You've had ample warning of the changes I'm going to make now the property is mine. There's no reason on earth why you couldn't all have looked round for some-where else to rent. If you'd had any forethought you'd have done that as soon as my company bought the site last year.'

'In this town?' She loosed a peal of laughter. 'How do you imagine any of us can afford the rents they're asking in the centre of town? Only the big chains can pay that sort of money! And anyway, can you honestly see my sort of shop in a brand new purpose-built box? Antiques belong in an old building like this, one with character, not some hideous, modern, featureless "retail unit"——'

'I can assure you my architects are creative, sensitive people who wouldn't know a box if they saw one. But you've made your point. Do I take it you're now open to discussing this with me?' Before she could answer, he said, 'I'll pick you up after work this evening. Nobody in this town has engagements at that time. And if you're going on somewhere later I'll have the car drop you off.'

'For goodness' sake! Don't you imagine I can organise my life without help from you?'

'No,' he replied with a deliberate smile. 'I think you need all the help I can give you.'

'Of all the arrogant——' But before she could say anything else he had swivelled and was heading towards the door. She saw him bend his dark head to read the times of opening and closing on the printed card on the glass, then he was outside, and she saw him walk off down the street without a backward glance.

★   ★   ★

'He's utterly beyond reason!' she fumed moments later to Jenni who ran the flower shop next door as she flung herself down in a chair behind the counter and rapidly explained what had happened. All she omitted was a reference to the way her heart had begun to gallop with the impetuosity of a herd of wild horses when he had swept her with that all-seeing silvery grey stare. She was still angry about it. She gave Jenni a careful look. 'I expect he's been in here, trying to talk you round, hasn't he?' she demanded.

Jenni shook her head. 'No, but then I didn't stand up at the meeting last night and make speeches.' She grinned. 'You really roused the rabble, Emma. *La Passionara*! I don't know how you did it. You were brilliant. Just the shot in the arm the committee needs. And I always thought you were the shy type!'

'I am.' Emma frowned, then gave a little laugh. 'At least, I thought I was, but when I'm as threatened as I am now it's only common sense to forget all that and do one's utmost. Anyway,' she added, 'it would take more than Mr Cool to frighten me. He seems to think he can bulldoze his way into the community and we'll all welcome him with open arms.'

'Hmm,' replied Jenni, giving Emma a mischievous glance. 'I wouldn't mind opening welcoming arms to him, that's for sure. He's a raunchy devil. Pity he's the enemy.'

'He's the enemy all right—he's going to swallow us for supper if we let him. We're going to have to fight him every inch of the way.'

Emma wondered if she could leave early that evening, giving him the slip, but after a moment's reflection she realised it would only delay things. All afternoon she brooded in her office at the back of the shop, there being few customers to disturb her in late February with the rain lashing against the windows, and when it was time to close she made her way round on the stroke of six, switching on the burglar alarm, setting the timer for the lights in the window—and trying not to regard the sleek silver car that was drawing up outside the shop as a harbinger of doom.

'Round one, here we go!' she told herself as she turned the key in the lock and threw a glance across the pavement. He was uncoiling from within the recesses of the car and before she could move was loping across the pavement towards her like some predatory night animal, an enigmatic smile on his face that seemed to bode nothing but ill.

'Good,' he greeted her. 'I knew you'd be sensible. It's obvious you have the common sense of Capricorn. . .' he paused '. . .with the taste of Libra. . .' he paused again '. . .but if I was pushed to it I'd bet my last dollar on. . .' he weighed her with his glance, then gave her a sudden dazzle of a smile '. . .defensive, crabby creature, hiding the moon-lady inside. You simply have to be born under the sign of Cancer. . .' Laughing, he reached out and picked up the little silver crab, one of the many charms hanging from the delicate chain around her neck. 'Yes, I thought so, and a romantic like me. . .'

'We're the same sign?' She was incredulous at the thought that he was supposed to be some sort of mirror image, her face plainly showing how offensive she found that idea, but he laughed, shaking his head.

'I can see the idea horrifies you. But you needn't worry, I'm something else. Which one, you'll have to guess!'

'As if I'm interested,' she mocked. He was certainly something else in more senses than one! 'Anyway,' she continued, 'I thought you were supposed to be the big tycoon. Are you trying to say you have an astrologer on your payroll too?'

He threw back the dark head. 'It might not be a bad idea—at least it'd help us figure out what the opposition are up to!' Then, before she could draw back, he said, 'Before you start imagining I'm vulnerable to that sort of thing, I should explain that my sister was——' He frowned, then broke off, turning abruptly without bothering to finish what he'd been going to say. 'Come along, Miss Shields, we'd better get a move on. I've found somewhere where we can have a drink and if we're not clawing each other's eyes out by the time they serve dinner we can even stay and have a bite to eat.'

'I don't intend to make an evening of it,' Emma countered, curious to know what he had been on the brink of telling her. The fact that he had remembered their conversation of that afternoon, and had obviously been mulling it over, presumably with the intention of disarming her with his close attentions, made her feel confused again. But it intrigued her enough to start to ask questions about him, and the arm he placed casually around her waist as he guided her over to his car felt oddly protective.

She forced herself to remember how annoyed she was that he was doing his character analysis trick again. It was unpleasant to think he imagined she was an open book. He made her feel defenceless and she didn't like the feeling. She lapsed into an impenetrable silence as they drove along. If he thought he was going to get another thing out of her, he was wrong.

The inn he took her to was down a lane alongside the river. It was dark now but a full moon shone fitfully behind racing clouds. They had to run from the car into the porch of the inn because of the rain. He was laughing when he turned to look down at her. 'Did you get wet?'

'Just a little,' she admitted. He was brushing his hands over her damp hair, the gesture so light that he scarcely touched her, but even so her senses prickled with expectation. She managed to move back with a shake of the head as if trying to get rid of the water drops and his touch, all at the same time. But he caught her hands in his.

'You look marvellous, even coming out straight from work.' He fingered the edge of her velvet cape. 'Do you always wear such beautiful things?'

'People are always bringing antique clothes in to sell to me, things they've found in an attic, gowns their great-grandmothers wore. Sometimes they're irresistible. This is a Victorian evening cloak——' She held it out so he could see it properly in the porch light, then remembered who he was. 'I can't give you much time,' she told him with a lift of her chin. 'I have to get home.'

'Someone waiting for you?' he murmured just above her left ear.

She swung her head then wished she hadn't—his lips were only inches from her own. Before she could step back out of range he put an arm around her hips, preventing her escape. 'Well?' he whispered, transfixing her with a silvery stare.

'What has my private life to do with you?'

'Absolutely nothing—yet,' he told her with a smile, 'but it may have at some future date, depending on how things proceed this evening.'

'You arrogant devil!' she exploded.

'Touchy!' he mocked. 'Why does the thought bother you so much? Are you married?' He looked as if it wouldn't bother him one jot.

When she tried to swing away, he pulled her back so

that she was almost pinned in his arms and before she could struggle free he asked again, 'Well? Are you?' And when she didn't answer straight away he said roughly, 'It's not a State secret, is it? Surely you can tell me a little thing like that?'

She broke free. 'My personal life, Mr del Sarto, is absolutely nothing whatsoever to do with you. And no, it's not a State secret, merely an irrelevance. All right?'

He came between her and the door, preventing her from going in, and when she stepped back in astonishment at his rudeness he merely thrust it open and allowed her through with a flourish, a deliberate smile masking his true feelings. Inside she didn't doubt he was seething because she hadn't fluttered at his feet. It was obvious he had had his own way for far too long.

She stalked on ahead of him, conscious of the stares of the other customers at the bar, and aware that they must look an odd couple, almost like lovers who'd had a tiff. She tried to ignore the interested looks cast in their direction and turned to him. 'I'll have a Campari and soda,' she smiled, 'and then I must go.' Her eyes locked with his and she could see he had read the message. It said she wasn't a woman who was going to be pushed around.

His response was a brief glint of amusement as he went to the bar to order their drinks. It must be marvellous, she thought, to have his sort of power and to witness the lengths people would go to to please him. But he was in for a shock. She knew she and the rest of the shopkeepers in the block were going to find it hard to get their own way against a man like him. But they would fight him. They had to. She had to. It was life or death.

Sitting down at one of the tables, she began to fiddle nervously with her silver chain. How was she going to approach this? She was determined not to trust him, no matter how charming he proved to be—and she'd already seen how easily he could switch that charm on. It was obvious there was a reason for inviting her here this evening, if inviting was the right word—kidnapping was more appropriate. Merely to 'have a talk' was only part of it. There was something else, and she wondered if she was going to be able to stand up to him, or be mangled underfoot?

'Pensive?' He placed a glass in front of her and she jerked her head up as he slid down beside her.

It was an invitation to open herself to him, but instead she turned away. She could feel his eyes on her face as if he was trying to winkle out her secret thoughts.

'When do we decide to call a truce and start to talk?' he asked. 'I'm willing to be very frank with you. Very frank.'

Slowly she tilted her head towards him. 'Really, Mr del Sarto? You?' She allowed a small, mirthless smile to play around her lips. 'Frankness is the last thing I would expect from a man like you. There has been no evidence of that at all so far. If I played poker it certainly wouldn't be with an opponent like you. But I would remind you of one thing. Where my livelihood is at stake, you're going to find the game less of a walkover than you imagine. This is my pledge, Mr del Sarto: I shall fight you till the last breath.'

'Spoken like a true Cancerian,' he murmured with a mocking smile. 'When it comes to defending your own material interests there's nobody like you. Now, will you answer my question? Are you in fact married?' He lifted her left hand and, eyes never leaving her face, placed his lips lightly on the tips of her fingers, allowing them to touch, briefly, the thin silver ring on her fourth finger.

Emma felt a tremor of anger. Who did he think he

was, probing and prying as if he had a right to every last
detail of her private life? She longed to snatch her fingers
from out of the soft pressure of his own, but her will was
momentarily paralysed and all she could do was stare up
at him, like a creature transfixed by the light.

CHAPTER TWO

'LET'S get down to business,' Emma jerked out. 'That is why we're here, isn't it?' Her glance swept the romantic corner Mark had found for them. It seemed positively indecent to be talking business in such a setting with its soft lighting and intimate seating arrangement. He must have chosen it deliberately. To soften her up. She moved her knees a fraction to avoid his and gave him a glare.

'I love it when you pout,' he murmured. 'You're a very pretty woman, Miss Shields.'

'Business. You wanted to talk, you said. Presumably,' she went on with a burst of insight, and ignoring the husky drop in his tones, 'you're hoping you can get the low-down from me about the anti-del-Sarto faction?' She gave a hollow laugh. 'No chance, I'm afraid. I'm not that stupid.'

'So you see me as some kind of devious politician, winkling secrets out of the enemy? That's quite flattering—to think I could winkle anything out of you, Miss Crab.'

His grey eyes held a challenging glint that would have been dangerous to mistake for humour. It sent a shiver down her spine. Despite the apparent lightness of his manner she knew they were still at battle stations.

'You fence with me all the time,' she came back. 'I wish you'd stop. Let's lay our cards on the table. You said you wanted to be frank.'

'I thought you didn't want to listen.'

'You're infuriating!' The corners of her mouth turned

21

down again and she felt her eyes moisten with tears of
frustration. He was so hard. Underneath the charm he
was as hard as rock. She was beginning to see that she
was out of her depth. He knew exactly when to play soft
and when to show the iron fist. The husky tone he used
was deliberate. She mustn't imagine it meant what it
suggested. He was playing with her. Didn't take her
seriously. But it was a matter of her livelihood. Her
antiques business was precarious at the best of times;
now, with his threat to close her down, it made her feel
unbearably insecure. He must know how she felt. It was
sheer callousness that made him play sexy with her. As
if there was time for anything like that when the threat
of closure was moving closer day by day!

'Guessed my birth sign yet?' he murmured unexpec-
tedly, lifting her hand in his and holding it near his lips.

'I haven't given it a second thought. Can we get on?'
She pulled her hand free and drew something out from
between the V of her blouse. It was a pretty fob watch
dangling on a black velvet ribbon. Glancing at it, she
said, 'I really do have to go soon.' She sounded more
sensible than she felt. Already she could feel her heart
beating out of control, and she knew she was halfway to
wanting what the promise in his voice implied.

A delicious aroma was issuing from the kitchens and
an instant image of what it would be like to be wined
and dined by such a man swept over her. If he hadn't
been on the wrong side of the fence he would have been
an intriguing escort for the evening. It was so long since
she'd dated anyone. . .

He was reaching forward and lifting the little watch to
look at the back. Touching the scrolled pattern with the
tips of his fingers, he nodded as if it confirmed something
he already suspected. 'Pretty. Very original. Very you.'
His silvery eyes blazed over her face for a moment as if

with some strange knowledge in them. 'Well.' He let the watch swing back to nestle amid the lacy ruffles at the front of her blouse, and Emma trembled as the tips of his fingers grazed her skin. His manner switched instantly to business mode, however. 'The position is as you know. We bought that whole block with the idea of developing it. The city planning department were delighted to have a buyer. You must know it's been on the market for a long time, ever since the road-widening scheme was shelved.'

'Yes, I know.' Emma pulled herself together. 'The previous owners were bought out under a compulsory purchase order,' she said, marvelling at how cool she sounded. 'It was quite a scandal, so I've heard. But it all happened before I moved here——' She broke off and risked a darting glance from beneath her lashes.

He was still watching her, but closely, picking up on everything she said as if filing it away. Almost without a pause he asked, 'So how long have you lived here?'

Fielding his question, she came back, 'I took up the lease five years ago and it's taken all that time to build up my business to what it is today.'

He pretended not to notice that she hadn't given him a direct answer and instead remarked, 'So you've always known it would be a short-term tenancy?'

'I hoped when it changed hands something more permanent could be agreed. . .' She frowned and then decided to be frank. 'The insecurity's a constant worry. Of course it is. But I didn't know what else to do. I really had no choice. When I started up I had no capital——'

'So how did you get into antiques?'

'I don't see what that has to do with anything.'

'It has a lot to do with how I make my eventual decision——'

'I thought——'

'I need to have full knowledge of everything that's gone on——'

'But——'

'If you started with nothing, even though paying only a peppercorn rent, you've done remarkably well. There were some valuable objects in that little shop of yours——'

'Thank you,' she replied with asperity. 'You're an expert on antiques as well as property, are you?'

'I recognise quality when I see it.' His expression was enigmatic. Emma felt her glance held by the depth of the look he gave her. A blush began to spread over her cheeks. His expression told her clearly that he was referring to herself! How dared he? Was she supposed to find it flattering to be judged like this?

She leaned back against the upholstered seat and said, 'I resent being classed as just another object to be evaluated, Mr del Sarto. I'm a businesswoman. A successful one, though by your standards I'm obviously worth only peanuts. I find everything about you thoroughly objectionable. If we're here to discuss some proposal you have to make, then let's get on with it. You can cut out the compliments, if that's what you imagine they are, as I only find that sort of thing insulting. What is it you have to say to me?'

'Shall we see what's on the menu?'

She blinked. 'Sorry?'

He gave a brief smile. 'I don't know about you, but I only had chance to snatch a sandwich at midday. Let's eat now so we can talk things over in a civilised fashion and then——'

'I've told you. I have to get home.'

'The husband?'

'There is no hus——' Too late she realised he'd

inserted his former question and she'd given him the answer he was after. She blushed, angry with herself, gritting her teeth under a dismissive smile. 'I would simply prefer not to waste a whole evening on something which is obviously going to end in disagreement,' she clipped. 'If you hope to find out what our strategy is, as I've already said, you haven't a hope.'

'Strategy? That's a strong word. So you really see this as all-out war?'

'Isn't it?'

'I hadn't looked at it like that.'

'I suggest you try to.'

He raised two black eyebrows at this.

'None of us intends to give in,' she added for good measure.

His square-cut jaw seemed to tighten a fraction, but there was no other expression on his face and his eyes were empty of any clue as to what he felt. One wrist, swathed in gold, lifted to beckon a hovering waiter. 'I haven't booked,' he said when the boy approached. 'Can you find me a table for two?'

Emma froze with annoyance. When the waiter left she said, 'So you're not dining alone this evening after all? I thought you said you were.' She began to pull the folds of her cloak round her with the obvious determination to leave.

'No,' he replied in a surprisingly husky voice, 'don't go. I'm not dining alone. . . at least, I hope I'm dining with Emma Shields.' He made her name sound like a caress. 'Please, Emma——' He broke off, and the briefest smile flitted across his face. 'Let's stop fencing, as you see it, and try to find some common ground.'

'I'm afraid there isn't any, Mr del Sarto,' she said, pointedly brushing off the intimacy of that sudden 'Emma'. 'There can be no common ground between us.

We so obviously come from different worlds.' She felt her heart contract. There was a miasma of pain around it. But what she said was true and had to be faced.

'Different worlds?' He gave a burning glance. 'Do we, indeed? And how do you know that?'

'It's too obvious.' She sat back for a moment. Her hands were trembling. She had a sudden urge to run them over and over through his black hair.

But he was shaking his head. 'I feel we've probably got more in common than you'd like to admit. I know when I set eyes on you last night—well, what can I say?' He looked into the distance. 'I felt an affinity for you, even though I think you were mistakenly pitching against me. We're not on opposite sides of the fence at all, you know. I hoped I could prove that to you this evening.' He looked full into her eyes and Emma faltered.

She felt her intention to leave begin to ebb. It was only right to give him a fair hearing, came the voice of reason, and, if he really did have some sort of compromise in mind, maybe she ought to stay and listen? She didn't want to lose her shop, and if there was the smallest chance of hanging on to it, well, she'd be stupid to throw it away out of sheer pigheadedness.

Taking advantage of her momentary indecision, he leaned forward. 'We are very much the same type of people. I trust my intuition and it's never let me down. Will you trust me?'

'Trust you?' She gulped. 'That's a lot to ask on a first meeting.'

He nodded. 'I know it is. Save your answer until you know me better.' He covered one of her hands in his. There was a smile on his face, his eyes luminous, looking at her softly.

Doubting that fate would put it in their way to get to know each other any more intimately than as landlord and tenant, she couldn't help giving a slight nod. 'Trust doesn't really come into it,' she told him. 'Any agreement worth anything would have to be properly drawn up by our solicitors.'

His glance slid away. 'You're very businesslike. But let's not rush things. You may not want what I have to offer.' He turned back with another smile, but this time his expression was different.

'Well, is it worth my while staying or not?' she exclaimed, wondering what that look meant. 'I thought the purpose of dining together was to thrash out some mutually agreeable compromise?'

'This is an exploratory meeting,' he corrected, his eyes blank. 'I don't have enough facts to be able to come up with anything useful to you at the moment. You'll have to be patient and, as I've said, I need you to be open with me.'

Emma bit her lip and looked down at the table. Her suspicions were being first calmed, then aroused. He was impossible to read. She would simply have to keep quiet until she saw what game he was playing. One thing she would have to remember, and that was to guard against the beginnings of an irrational desire to trust him. Damn it, he seemed to be on the level. Was it only her naturally suspicious Cancerian nature that wouldn't let go of its doubts? There was something about him that said, Yes, I'm a man of my word. But he hadn't made any promises, and she still didn't know what he was after. This dinner invitation was obviously designed to be more than just a business discussion.

Just then the waiter returned. Surprise, surprise! thought Emma, when she heard that a table had been made ready for them. Mark del Sarto gave a complacent smile. He had obviously expected nothing less. Then he drew back her chair and led her into the dining-room.

It was a restaurant she had always wanted to visit, but since Tom's illness dining out had always been difficult. Besides, the sheer expense was enough to put her off. It was, unfortunately, the sort of place, too, where an attractive male escort was an essential requirement. . . Her frown at that thought changed to a smile. At least Mark del Sarto fitted the bill there! He caught sight of that sudden lift at the corners of her mouth as she turned to look at him.

'That's better,' he observed, touching her on the shoulder. 'You have the wickedest smile. But I won't ask what wayward thought strayed into your mind just then!' He placed himself across the table from her and she felt his eyes on her as she picked up the menu and flicked it open, staring with furious concentration at the jumbled letters in front of her. In a moment he would tell her what sort of deal he was offering and whether it would mean a reprieve for her or not. He obviously liked playing cat and mouse, taking things in his own time, and she would have to be patient. If he was taken in by her frilly blouse and flowing, feminine clothes and thought they meant she wasn't capable of looking after her own business interests, that was his problem.

Forcing all that aside for the minute, she scanned the menu more confidently. Apart from the sense of imminent disaster he represented, this could all be extremely pleasant.

'Do you like seafood?' he asked. 'I recommend the lobster. The chef has his own very simple recipe.' He went on to suggest one or two other things but she plumped for his first suggestion.

'Not because I can't make up my own mind,' she murmured with a half-smile, 'but because I happen to like it.'

'It's compatible with your birth sign, anyway. But I

hope it also means you're beginning to trust my judge-ment?' He eyed her with amusement.

'I don't doubt your judgement,' she replied. 'You wouldn't be where you are if you didn't know what you were doing!'

His eyes narrowed suggestively. 'I certainly wouldn't,' he agreed. His glance silvered over her with a total lack of ambiguity.

She felt herself flush scarlet and managed to mumble, 'I dare say I can allow myself to trust your recommen-dations in the matter of cuisine.' When she raised her chin, the blush had gone and the challenge in her smile was enough to show she meant just that: she would trust him this far and no further.

'Usually two people in our situation would have a pleasant chat about themselves,' he said, with a change of tone, 'but I suspect I'm going to run up against the barbed-wire fence if I try that with you, so let me tell you about my company instead.' He paused. 'I have nothing to hide.'

She opened her mouth to deny that she had anything to hide either, but the waiter came up and as soon as they had ordered he began at once. 'We're a construction company first and foremost, and as you probably know I won the tender for the new marina and residential complex down by the old quay recently. That's how I come to be operating in this area. It's actually a very convenient location from which to run a business, being close to several airports and with good road and rail links. The way things are in London, I may relocate here at some point.' He paused and frowned. 'But it's early days yet. We'll see how things shape up.'

She watched him carefully. There was nothing in his expression to tell her who he meant by 'we'—whether his company, or a more personal connection. She frowned at her plate, wondering whether or not she dared ask him, or whether it would be to risk the sort of rebuff she had dealt him in response to a similar question. She felt him lean forward to peer more closely into her face.

'Yes?'

His eyes rested gently on her upturned face.

'I was wondering if you always referred to yourself in the plural,' she hazarded.

He gave her a silvery smile. 'Not always.'

Not sure whether to take this as the expected rebuff or not, she waited for him to go on.

After a pause he said, 'No, I'm not married, if that's what you mean. And, unlike you, I don't mind admitting it.' He paused again and his eyes darkened as rapidly as a storm clouding the sea. 'No children. No ties.' He wiped the dark look from his face and she got the impression of a man forcing some deep emotion back into the inner recesses of his soul—or was it just her imagination that made her think that? Did he secretly want ties? Children even? It was impossible to tell.

His hand came out and picked up her own left hand, and his eyes sought and found the silver ring on her fourth finger. She snatched her hand from his grasp and belatedly concealed it under the tablecloth.

'I'm sorry,' he said. 'I shouldn't probe. You don't like it.' His expression darkened again.

Emma toyed with her glass. She couldn't tell what assumptions he had made, but she knew she couldn't talk about Tom just then. 'Perhaps it would be safer,' she said haltingly, 'if we kept strictly to business?'

Raising her face, she felt their glances mesh. Something seemed to fly between them and it was like walking down a long corridor to a forbidden destination—it was an invitation and a promise and she wanted to run towards him, to open the door into his secret world and to hold no secrets from him either. But there was something menacing in the air too; her courage failed her and she retreated as quickly as she could, jerking her head and pretending she hadn't noticed the beginnings of this strange event taking place between them. It was a marker in their relationship, but she drew back from it out of fear.

Giving an artificial laugh and unable to stop herself, she began to prattle on about something totally trivial until she felt safe enough to slow down and become herself again. At this obvious sign of retreat he lapsed into silence, and now he was looking at her with shuttered eyes. . . brooding. . . wintered.

To Emma it was like someone locking himself inside an ice fortress, and though they continued to talk of this and that, and on the surface everything continued as before, underneath, where it mattered, the mood had changed. Any feeling of intimacy had gone. Under the surface a barrier of ice had been erected. The voice of common sense warned her to remember that there could be no involvement between them; he was still the enemy, still the robber baron, and even now she didn't know whether he was going to decide to destroy her.

It wasn't until the end of the meal that he ventured to mention her shop again. 'You must be making enough money now to pay the sort of rent they're asking in the town centre?' he asked, assessing her reaction with a shrewd businessman's face. It was as if he was sitting inside a cloak of ice.

'Yes,' she admitted. 'but that would cut into my profit, wouldn't it? I'd have to put my prices up to stay at the same level.'

'What do the others feel? Are they all behind you?'

'Of course,' she replied at once. If he thought there

was any dissension among the small group of traders he would be sure to try to play on it.

'Why don't you all get together and make me an offer for the block?' he asked. 'I would sell it back to you at the going rate if that's what you really want.'

'You mean buy it?'

He nodded.

'We hadn't thought of that.'

'Why don't you?'

She gave a sudden mirthless laugh. 'So that's why you wanted to soften me up.' A flicker of disappointment ran through her. What a fool she was to imagine his interest was anything other than mercenary! She shrank back into her shell. 'Maybe you ought to meet everyone else and tell them what you suggest yourself. Though quite honestly I don't see most of them being able to afford the sort of figure you probably have in mind.' She managed to give a flippant shake of the head. 'I doubt whether even I could pay, and I'm probably the most successful in terms of turnover on the whole block.' She knew Jenni's little flower shop made only enough to scrape a modest living for Jenni and her widowed mother.

He let the matter drop. When the meal was over they lingered a little and Emma noticed that now he had sown the seeds of a plan in her mind he was willing to relax and put his efforts into charming her. It was almost a restoration of that earlier phase of intimacy when something beyond business had seemed to hang in the balance, and it disarmed Emma enough to prompt her to joke, 'So do you think I'm running true to type?'

A second Irish coffee brimming with double cream had been placed in front of her. After eating so well she was feeling better than she had done for a long time. Occasions like these had been out of the question for the past few years. Even though Tom encouraged her to go out and enjoy herself, she never did because it seemed unfair. But Mark was beginning to make her feel like a woman again. They seemed to get on really well so long as he didn't try to probe too deeply and she, in turn, avoided the darker side of his personality, that enigmatic blank she could not quite fathom.

It was only after a long pause that he offered a reply to her question. 'Type?' He wrinkled his brow.

'As someone born under the sign of Cancer,' she reminded him.

'Oh, that.' He looked thoughtful. 'When you've lived with someone who takes it seriously,' he said at last, 'you tend to develop certain expectations.' He gave a bantering smile. 'We're supposed to have a lot going for us.'

'We? Our signs—whatever yours is?' Whom had he lived with, then? Was he referring to his sister again? She played safe and asked instead, 'So what sign are you?'

He shook his head, continuing to smile. 'That's for you to find out.'

'Huh! So tell me what you expect, at least?' she joked with a toss of her head to hide her annoyance at his less than frank response.

'Nothing much,' he said, abruptly averting his head. 'Shall we go?'

Now she was the one left out on a limb with a crowd of unanswered questions buzzing in her head. He rose to his feet and came swiftly round the table to help her up. Feeling rebuffed, she decisively gripped the edge of her chair then slowly pulled herself upright. All right, Mr Cool, she was thinking with a bright, false smile on her face, play it this way. I don't care. Keep your secrets. Did he think she cared a damn? He should be so lucky! She'd only been trying to be friendly. The food and the wine and the way he'd deliberately tried to lull her had led her along paths she had no interest in following.

Scorning his outstretched arm, she made off towards the exit without waiting for him. Her only achievement was to find herself having to wait for him while he dealt with the bill.

'I'll drive you home,' he told her curtly when he eventually came up beside her.

'There's no need,' she replied ungraciously. 'I live close to the shop back in town. I can easily get a cab.'

'Don't be ridiculous.' Without waiting he gripped her by the elbow and steered her outside into the car park. It was still pouring with rain. The moon was deeply hidden behind banks of cloud.

'Thank you for a lovely meal,' she offered in distant tones when once they were seated inside his car.

The wipers swished back and forth as if measuring the seconds that were left to them. They seemed to be telling her how little time there was to put everything right. But it had all gone sour. There was nothing to be found in her heart that she could say to put things right, for there was nothing between them except business. Not even incipient friendship. Her earliest suspicions had been correct. He had simply wanted to test the ground so he could judge whether it would be useful to make his tenants an offer. The charm, the glittering smile, had all been part of his strategy to get information out of her.

Eyeing his hard profile as he drove back through the rain-drenched streets, she even began to doubt whether it was a serious offer at all. Maybe he was just taking care of his public image? If it got out that he had been willing to negotiate—but that, of course, the protesters were unable to meet his asking price—he would come out of it looking like the public benefactor he wished to appear.

As the car pulled up outside the row of houses close to where she lived, he turned to her. 'Emma, you're extremely deep in thought. I do hope you've changed your opinion about me. There is no need for this trench warfare, you know. If it really came to a showdown, you and your friends would be annihilated. It would be best to try to do a deal with me.'

'Thanks for the warning. I guess it's back to square one.' She made as if to open the car door but he reached across and put one hand over hers, staying her fingers; then, as they both became aware at the same moment of each other's closeness, he turned, lips grazing her cheek, before drawing his head back and giving her that enigmatic, all-seeing scrutiny that had already unnerved her.

She felt the heartbeat of anger quicken against him and just had time to mutter a hoarse protest before his lips came marauding down over her own, nothing of gentleness in them, just a blind possession that took her breath away. Abruptly he lifted his head. He too was breathing heavily.

'I didn't mean that,' he grated. 'Goodnight.' With one movement he pressed the lock on the door and opened it, and she found herself automatically climbing out.

For a moment she stood in the rain in a confusion of astonished anger. Then she slammed the door between them, not caring if his fingers were in it or not, and headed blindly along the pavement towards the front gate of her house.

She became aware of his car purring into life, then it came creeping slowly along beside her out of the darkness. She turned, prepared to see him gun off down the road, but instead he brought it to a velvety halt. She watched him climb out.

He strode round the front of the car and gripped her

by both shoulders. 'I thought you said you lived just here?'

She glanced up the road towards the house. 'I do.'

'Which one?'

'The one with the light on.'

He noted the lighted front steps in the middle of a pretty row of Victorian houses about fifty yards away.

'Why did you ask me to stop just here, then? Afraid I'd see where you live?' His eyes narrowed suspiciously. 'Or is it that you don't want whoever's waiting for you to hear the car?'

'Leave me alone! It's nothing to do with you!'

Rain swept in an icy gust across their faces. She felt his fingers bite into her shoulder and her knees seemed as if they were about to buckle but he shook her once then released her with a hard smile. 'Go in. I want to know you're safe inside. I don't care a damn where you live. Only whether you get back safely. And if you've any explaining to do once you get in I'm sure your natural charm will see you through. Go on.'

He turned her round and pushed her towards the light. Puzzled by the fierceness in a face that was usually so enigmatic, Emma stumbled away, the hood of her cloak lifted against the rain until she came to the laurel bushes beside the front gate. She gave one hurried backward glance, then fled to safety up the short path to the six steps to the front door. A light blazed rainbow colours all over them and with a little cry of relief she inserted the key, spun the lock and let herself inside without another glance.

She could sense his brooding presence, his eyes clinging on to her until the very moment she slammed the door between them.

At once a masculine voice welcomed her from an inner room, warmth and love evident in its very tones. 'Emma!

You're late!' came the reproof with a hint of a chuckle in it. 'Have you had a nice time?'

She gave a small cry and pushed open the door to the room beyond.

CHAPTER THREE

THE fair hair of the young man sitting in an armchair with a rug wrapped round his legs glinted with the lustre of a halo against the firelight. It was a cosy scene, the rose-pink of the furnishings giving a welcome glow that lifted Emma's heart immediately. The sinister shape of the man standing outside on the pavement in the rain seemed to be a figure from a different world.

She crossed the room and kissed its occupant on the top of the head. 'Did you manage all right without me, Tom?'

He reached up and squeezed her elbow. 'Course I did. You'd left everything perfectly within reach and you didn't forget a thing, not even the mango pickle.'

'I thought I could smell curry. Is that what you had?'

He nodded. 'Valerie popped in and prepared the rice for me. She's an angel, that woman,' he added, smiling up into Emma's concerned face. 'Don't worry, love. You need to get out. It's all right.'

Emma bit her lip and turned away, her mood spoilt slightly by fresh worries. She went to stand beside the high Victorian mantelpiece and rested her chin on her forearm. A gilt mirror, much like the one in the shop, reflected her own pensive face back to her. Behind her the room gleamed and glowed. It was her haven, an Aladdin's cave, full of the objects most precious to her, where she could retreat from the world to a place of safety. Not least in importance in that place was Tommy.

She turned. 'I won't leave you, you know.' The silver ring she wore was reflected in the mirror as she drummed

38

her fingers up and down on the rose-pink marble mantelshelf as if she had been contradicted. 'I mean it. You needn't make those noises at me!' She smiled tenderly and added, 'If you want rid of me you're going to have to find a substitute. I won't go otherwise!'

'Silly chicken.' He reached out for her again and pulled her towards him, slipping his arms round her waist and burying his head in the lace between her breasts. It might have been erotic in other circumstances, but there was something so brotherly, almost childlike in the gesture that Emma could only smile and bend her head to press her lips against his fine fair hair.

'So,' he mumbled after a moment, 'how did it go? Did you charm the big bad wolf into leaving you alone?'

She made a face. 'Nope.'

'You sounded rather harassed when you phoned and told me you were going to have a talk with him. I've been speculating all evening on what you've actually been saying to each other. Surely he didn't just want to tell you again what came out at the meeting last night?'

'More or less.' She frowned and went to lean against the mantelpiece again. 'Honestly, Tom, I don't understand him. He's an enigma, to say the least. I can't quite fathom him, though on one level I feel as if——' She broke off.

'As if what, my love?'

'Oh, I don't know.'

'He certainly seems to have shaken you.'

'What do you mean?' Her head jerked up.

Tom laughed softly. 'Is he handsome, this guy?'

'What on earth makes you ask a thing like that?' Her cheeks crimsoned and she turned in case he noticed, but he was too sharp for her.

'Wealthy men often have a kind of sexual charisma——'

'Tommy!'

But he was chuckling to himself. 'Your face is a dead giveaway, darling. I love to see you blush. Tell me about him. Come on, sit beside me.' He patted his legs. Ruefully Emma slid to the Axminster and rested her head against his knees.

'Did the physio come today?' she asked, stroking the plaid rug and aware of a familiar pang when she felt the weak limbs beneath.

Tom nodded. 'She's a poppet. I'm blessed with the attentions of some wonderful women.'

'Me included, even though I leave you alone all evening?'

'Definitely you included.' He stroked her hair. 'But don't sidetrack. Tell me about this guy who makes you blush.'

'He does not!' She shook off his soothing fingers. 'You're not to start imagining things, Tommy. I won't have it!'

'You have to move on, you know. This situation won't last forever.'

Emma felt tears fill her eyes but she averted her head so that Tommy wouldn't see. For a moment the lump in her throat was so huge that she couldn't speak, and she hoped he would believe she was merely lost in thought. She tried to block out the future as often as possible, to make these years remaining to them both as perfect as she could, but Tom was a realist and he never allowed her to forget that his time was circumscribed by the disease that was slowly paralysing him. Often he referred to the likelihood that he might get worse yet cling on to life for decades, unable to wash and dress himself, a helpless invalid. There was no self-pity in this. He was prepared for what lay ahead and tried to make Emma see it too. But she refused to think about the future, preferring instead to remember how it had once been for them both in the days now gone when they had first met and fallen in love.

For it hadn't always been this way. When he was twenty-three and she a mere nineteen, it had seemed as if the whole world lay before them. It was the beginning of love. Then Tom had become ill. For the first few months after the nature of his disease had been diagnosed he was in a fever of despair. It was then that he had asked Emma to become engaged. It had seemed the natural progression for them, but that was all of six years ago. She had been twenty by then. And she had felt so desperately sorry for her courageous Tom that she had said yes at once without a thought of the future.

She had made careful plans for them both, knowing that if they married it might only be for a short time and that it would be a marriage in name only. Practical by nature, she had plotted their financial future carefully, deciding that it would be up to her to see to all that sort of thing when he became too ill to work.

Things had moved quickly after that—Tom got suddenly worse, Emma took a lease on the shop, crammed it with what she frankly saw as junk until she could begin to stock it with more precious antiques, and mentally earmarked the gown she would wear on their wedding-day, at the same time checking out likely property so they could live close enough to the shop, so she could work and look after Tom properly as he became more and more helpless. But it was at this point that Tom had shown the firmness of character that later enabled him to survive the emotional trauma of that first year of illness.

'I'm not going to marry you, Emma,' he told her one night. 'Not because I don't love you, but because I could never stand in the way of your long-term happiness.

You're turning into a beautiful woman and you deserve a proper husband and lots of gorgeous babies. You'd become a sort of prisoner with me, locked in this half-life of mine, if we married. I love you too much to do that to you.'

She had been furious and marshalled every argument she could think of—of course they must marry; she loved him, didn't he know that? And she had found a perfect house for them at a price they could afford. And she had already chosen the gown she would wear on the day.

He had smiled at that. 'I'm sorry, but still no.'

'But we belong together,' she'd said in bewilderment.

'I didn't say we couldn't live together,' he had told her, as if to soften the blow of refusing anything more.

Initially she had recoiled at the idea of living with a man without the sanction of marriage vows. He'd talked her round. 'See me as a kind of lodger,' he'd said, adding brutally, 'I'm no use to you in the marriage department. Sex is out. I'm a cripple, Emma. See me for what I am.'

She had blazed with anger; in fact, it was their only disagreement in six years. But Tom had been adamant. 'The future belongs to you, my love. My life is here and now. If you'll share it with me for a time it'll be more than I have a right to expect.'

She had cried remorselessly, raging against the injustice of fate, but she had been forced to accept his wishes. There had been one or two men in her life along the way since then, meetings usually engineered by Tom himself, but there had been no one important enough to tear her away from the brother-sister love she now shared with him. He was her first love, and secretly she believed he would be her last.

Surreptitiously wiping a corner of her eye on the hem of her skirt, she said lightly now, 'You're very interested in Mark del Sarto. I hope you're not still trying to marry me off. I've told you it won't work! And certainly not to a man like him! He's the last man on earth, I'm afraid. He's so——' she shivered '—he's got a very dark side. I can't quite explain it.'

Tom stroked her hair. 'Well, you needn't get involved. It's not a prerequisite!' He laughed.

'All I have to do is make sure the shop and our future are secure.'

'What do you think will happen next?'

She went into details later on, over cocoa and biscuits, about the offer Mark del Sarto had made, and then she tried to explain her misgivings about it, until at Tom's insistence she sat by the phone and rang round all the people on the committee and told them what had happened. Reception to her news was mixed. Jenni was resigned. 'There's no way I could ever raise the cash and I'm sure the bank wouldn't give me a loan.' One or two of the others were more hopeful. The hairdresser and the man who ran the fruit shop resolved to take the offer seriously. Others were doubtful but determined to fight on.

After her last call she put the phone down with a sigh. 'There's nothing else I can do. We'll just have to wait and see what happens.'

Tom reached for one of the books propped within arm's reach. 'I don't believe in waiting and seeing,' he said. 'What do the stars say?' He flicked open an ephemeris.

Emma remained silent. It was since his illness that Tom had begun to take an interest in astrology. She saw it as a way of trying to make sense of the apparent randomness of destiny. It was as if he was trying to grasp at something solid, something that would reveal a meaning to what had happened to him and perhaps also suggest a glimmer of hope.

Now he said, 'You've got four planets passing through your opposite sign this month. Mercury, Saturn, Uranus and Neptune. . . Well, forewarned is forearmed.'

He mulled things over for a short while, then went on, 'It means you're not likely to see eye to eye with partners or close companions and you'll feel you don't receive all the support you deserve.'

'Really?' She wasn't giving him her full attention. Already her mind had gone back to that afternoon when Mark del Sarto had made those provoking remarks about her sun sign. Of course he couldn't have guessed she was Cancer just by intuition alone. He had spotted the little silver crab on a chain round her neck with those sharp grey eyes of his. He had then made a simple deduction. After all, it stood to reason, if his sister had been into that sort of thing—why the past tense? she wondered—that he couldn't fail to recognise the twelve signs. Idly she wondered what sign he was himself. As if she could care less!

Tom turned. 'Frowning?'

'That man,' she admitted. 'He makes me frown. He makes me spit flame, in fact. I was just wondering what sign he was. No doubt he'll be something nasty like Scorpio!' she exclaimed.

'Now, then,' admonished Tom equably, 'there are no nasty signs. There's good in all of them.'

'You would say that, Mr Libra. Always so reasonable, aren't you? At least he's definitely not one of you lovely balanced types willing to see everybody else's point of view! He can only see his own!'

'If he were Scorpio he'd be a good match for you. You'd have enough in common that you could understand each other, and enough differences that you'd have a lively time of it!' His eyes gleamed. 'Especially in bed!'

'Tom! Stop this!' She pretended to joke, but his words

sent a *frisson* of something like terror down her spine.
Mark del Sarto would annihilate her if she ever ventured
that close to him. She recalled the very phrase he had
used in another context. When he was talking about the
property problem he'd said, 'if it really came to a
showdown you and your friends would be annihilated.'
They would too. She knew it in the depths of her soul.

He came striding into the shop soon after she opened
next morning. In a long, belted raincoat in a masculine
shade of blue-grey to match the rain slashing against the
windows, he seemed to dwarf Emma as she rose hurriedly from her cushioned chair in the back room and
came to the door. She halted as he suddenly bulked in
front of her, blocking her exit into the shop. She thought
he was going to knock her over as he came charging up,
but he came to an abrupt stop within a few feet of her.
His face was wan, as if he had been awake all night, and
his eyes were as grey and blank as slate.

'You talked your way out of trouble last night, did
you?' he began without any sort of formal greeting.

'Good morning,' she replied frostily, face as impassive
as his own. She ignored his question and asked in the
same frigid tones, 'Are you here as a customer or in some
other capacity?'

He jerked back as if she had struck him and his lips
curled into the shadow of a smile. 'Oh, I'm being
reprimanded for forgetting my manners, am I? Good
morning, Miss Shields,' he mocked. 'Now, what about
answering my question?'

'Last night and what I did has nothing to do with
you.'

'As communicative as ever, true to type.' He flexed
his shoulders. 'Well two can play that game. Why do
you imagine I'm here?'

He gave her a direct look and she blurted before she could stop herself, 'To pressure me into some lousy agreement to move out?'

'You think so?'

'Aren't you?'

'And if I'm not?'

She shook her head. Suddenly her lips refused to open. It was monstrous the way he seemed to destroy her confidence with one look from those empty eyes. They seemed to be threatening something, as if to say he could devour her soul. She swayed, fighting back the feverish imaginings that were suddenly storming over her. It was unfair, she told herself again and again, as she tried to get a grip on reality. He shouldn't come barging in on her before she had properly started the day. The tension seemed to reach explosion point as he continued to regard her with a half-smile that was nothing if not enigmatic.

At length he pronounced one word. 'Wrong.' Then his face broke into a dazzle of white teeth, his cheekbones chiselled by such a smile to form an image of masculine good looks that made Emma's heart lose a beat.

She swayed again. What was happening to her? She loved Tom, but it didn't feel like this. But what was she saying? She felt only terror now at the premonition of something fearful hovering over her. Something sweeping her out of control. Despite his smile she was gasping with fright.

He reached out and seemed about to take her by the shoulder, but she stepped back with a flurry of movement, knocking a picture askew as she brushed the wall to escape him.

'Are you all right?' The dark head bent as he peered into her face.

Feeling foolish and at a loss to understand what had come over her, she gave a quick nod.

He prolonged his smile in a way that struck Emma as predatory. 'I'm sorry I startled you. Can we talk, or are you "busy" again?'

She felt as if she were falling, with nothing between her and the bottom of an endless black pit. 'It's not you who startled me,' she lied. 'It's just—I was miles away. Thinking about some furniture I have to go and see some time. I don't think I have any more room here at present, but maybe I can move things around. Of course, if I have to get out. . .' She let her words trail away with a sudden lack of conviction. His silvery glance had an element of scepticism in it, as if he could tell she was flustered and trying vainly to talk her way out of something. But what she said was true. She had scarcely got around to working out the practical problems of a change of premises. He wasn't to know the real reason she was shaking and gibbering like a complete idiot.

'Listen, you can carry on as usual. Business as usual, all right?' He said it again, as if unsure whether her dazed expression meant she didn't understand what he was saying. 'These things take months to arrange,' he went on. 'The council have to see the final plans and look them over before they can even start to arrive at a decision. I'm in no hurry to move you out. I've got too many other projects needing attention right now.'

'Lucky me. So that's why I've got a breathing-space? Are they similar to this? Pushing little people out of business?' She saw his eyes cloud as soon as the words were uttered. He was impassive when he said, 'I suppose you would see it like that.' He paused, his expression non-committal. 'Listen——' his manner changed '—I came in to see if you'd——' He broke off, then swivelled away into the shop.

Curious, she watched to see what he would do. He went over to a cabinet and picked up an ornament at random, looking underneath it to read the mark, then replacing it in the exact place it had originally been displayed. He seemed almost uncertain of himself, and she wondered what was making him react like this. Why was he here, anyway? And why couldn't he get straight to the point? It seemed out of character for a man like him to be unsure of himself.

She watched him move down one of the aisles to a group of gilt chairs arranged around an Edwardian card-table. He ran a finger thoughtfully over the glossy surface. The tiny gesture, sensual, deliberate, sent a shiver coursing over her as if the contact had trailed erotically over her own naked skin instead.

Lifting his head as if a decision had been made, he came back to where she was still rooted in the doorway of the back office.

'What do you do about deliveries?' he asked.

'Of what?' she looked puzzled.

He nodded over his shoulder. 'I'd like that table. Can you deliver it?'

She nodded. 'It'll be a small extra charge.' The brother of the man who ran the fruit shop had a large van and gave Emma a good discount on any jobs she gave him. In return she bought all her fruit and veg from his brother. It was all very friendly.

'Good.' He was fishing inside an inner pocket and brought out a bundle of notes. 'How much?'

'I—I—' Her normal acumen had disappeared completely. 'It's quite a nice piece,' she began.

'No need to do your sales patter. I'm buying. How much?'

'Three seventy-five including delivery.'

'Three fifty?' He began to peel some notes off. 'No, on second thoughts, I won't haggle with you.'

'Good,' she flushed. 'I wasn't about to accept less than three sixty.'

'With delivery?'

She nodded.

'It's a pretty little piece.' There was a gleam in his eyes as if he meant something else and she flushed angrily, but he carried on with a smooth, 'Here's the address. My phone number's there at the bottom. Call me?'

Her eyes opened blankly. 'Call you?'

'If you want to.' He turned abruptly and gave the table a glance, then started for the door. 'When can I expect it?'

'What?' she said stupidly, watching him go with the feeling of having been knocked over by a bus.

'The table, Miss Shields, the table.'

'Oh.' She gathered her wits. 'Will tomorrow do?'

He raised one hand in agreement and left. She watched the bell above the door jangle up and down then die to a whisper before giving a last silent spasm. When it finally came to a stop she turned without being aware of what she was doing and slumped down into a chair. Only after a good twenty seconds did her breathing return to something like normal. Her nerves felt as jangled as the bell, and when she came to open her sales ledger she found her writing spidering all over the place because her hand was shaking so much.

'I feel terrible,' she complained to Jenni when she popped next door for a break in an otherwise uneventful morning. 'That monster came in first thing and bought a table just like that, then swept out again. He makes me feel so angry! There's something so arrogant about him. Honestly, Jenni, I could throttle him or something.'

'Or something,' grinned Jenni. 'Yes, I can well understand that!'

'Oh, please, not you as well! I had enough with Tom making sly remarks about the sexual charisma of Scorpio man. He's probably something entirely different anyway. Just because he's reasonably good-looking and obviously loaded, everybody assumes. . .' She didn't outline what it was they assumed, but instead gave a tiny shrug that spoke volumes. 'I'd rather live with a rattlesnake than a man like that. And believe me, I haven't the slightest interest in any man except Tom.'

Jenni gave a knowing grin. But then her expression altered. 'And when——' She paused delicately. 'I mean, I know it seems hard, but later, in a few years' time, won't you regret letting chances slip through your fingers?'

'Has Tom been on the phone to you?' Emma's suspicions were aroused at once.

'I ring him once a day for a good chat. You know that, Emma. He's so sweet. I also have to get my readings from him. He's always spot-on.'

'You surely don't believe all that nonsense? I can understand poor Tommy taking it a little bit seriously, but *you*?'

'It sort of gives me hope.' Jenni frowned. 'I can't imagine living like this forever.' She glanced round the small shop. 'Something's got to change!'

'It'll change quick enough if del Sarto has his way. You'll be out on your ear like the rest of us.' Emma glared grumpily at an innocent-looking bunch of cut flowers and gave a huge sigh. She hadn't managed to get around to telling Jenni what was in her heart and now the opportunity seemed to have gone. But what was there to say anyway? That she became a total nincompoop the minute Mark del Sarto came within spitting distance? It was simply rage, she knew that. Simple apoplectic rage at his cold, calculating intention to do them all out of business.

'Trench warfare,' she said, turning away. 'He's promised to annihilate us. That's the word he used. That monster. What are we going to do?' She picked up a fallen rosebud, looked thoughtfully down at it and said, 'I'm going to get everybody together again, Jenni. We've got to make a proper plan. Maybe get some publicity for ourselves in the local Press. If enough people were organised against him, surely he wouldn't be able to go ahead?'

Jenni nodded. 'I'll help. Where and when?'

'My place, then Tom can join in. He's good at solving problems and seeing the other side to everything. Maybe he'll be able to predict which way del Sarto is going to go.'

'Let's do it soon. What about tomorrow?'

Emma nodded. 'Good idea. I'll get on the phone to everybody right away. Luckily trade's slack at the moment. It'll give me something to do!' Both women smiled. Emma found it difficult to express how much Jenni's support meant to her. Instead of saying anything, she tossed the rosebud on to the counter and made for the door. 'I'll see you later.'

It was cold in the shop with only a single-bar electric fire to huddle over, and by five o'clock Emma decided to call it a day. After ringing round the other committee members, there had only been one or two browsers but no customers to speak of, so she shrugged on the thick woollen coat she usually wore when she wasn't going anywhere special and gathered up her shopping. She had just switched out the lights and was groping her way towards the front of the shop, guided by the light in the

window, when a black shape hulked on the other side of
the glass panel. Typical, she thought with an inward
groan, a customer just when I'm about to go home. Then
she gave a gasp when she recognised the now familiar
face on the other side.

As she couldn't just stand looking out at him, she
opened the door.

'Deserting your post, Miss Shields?' came a lazy voice
from out of the shadows.

'It's raining too hard. Nobody's going to browse round
an antiques shop on a day like this,' she responded
irritably. Why had he come back? 'If you're wondering
why your table hasn't been delivered——'

'Heavens, no, I'm not in that much of a hurry.' He
laughed softly. 'I just happened to be passing and
wondered what you were doing.'

'I'm going home, as you can see.'

'I'll walk with you.' By now she was standing in the
street, the key already in her hand, and he snapped
open a large golfing umbrella and held it over her
head.

'Really, there's no need,' she protested, despite a
feeling that it would be futile to offer any resistance as
he was giving the usual impression of assuming he had a
right to his own way.

She gave the door a push to make sure it was properly
locked, then swivelled. Standing together underneath
the umbrella seemed to cut them off from the rest of the
world and put them on an intimate island of their own.
To give greater emphasis to their isolation, he tilted the
umbrella so that they were shielded from the sight of
anyone walking by.

'Emma,' he began huskily, 'have you been thinking
about what happened last night?'

Suddenly she was shuddering. He seemed to threaten

with the sheer physical power he possessed, but she couldn't step back out of danger, she couldn't get out, there was nowhere to run to. Her lashes came down, veiling her eyes, and she felt her body turn to an unresponsive block. With chilling deliberation he reached for her, lifting her chin and gazing silently into her face. There was no need for words. His brooding look said more than words ever could, hinting at something mysterious, still hidden. It sent tremors coursing through her. But what it was or what it meant she dared not imagine. Maybe it *was* simply anger that made her tremble so much when he came near.

'Last night,' he said in a voice grown unaccountably hoarse, 'I told you I didn't mean to kiss you.' He paused, then with an effort went on, 'It was a lie. I meant to kiss you from the first moment I set eyes on you. Before I knew your name. Before I knew anything about you. I saw you at the meeting, then the very next day I caught sight of you through the window while you arranged some things, though you didn't know I was there. What I should have said last night was, I hadn't meant to kiss you just then. Like that. Not when we were feeling less than friendly towards each other.'

As he spoke he began to slide his fingers back and forth over the silky skin under her jawbone. Then one thumb of the same hand came up and caressed the shallow hollow of her right cheek. It travelled from there to a corner of her mouth, then feathered in an exploratory arc over her parted lips. His forefinger probed at the edge of her mouth, forcing her lips back and parting her teeth, and as her head tilted in a desire to get away he inclined his head so that his own lips, his own parted lips, were only inches from her own.

He murmured her name once, then sank them again to that place they seemed to know from another life, and she was dizzied into a whirl of sensation, fire and ice running in simultaneous confusion over every nerve of her quivering frame.

Rain was pattering endlessly on the umbrella he held in one hand, and with the other, the one that had first taught her the unforgettable sensation of his touch, he began to caress the back of her head, tangling his fingers in the sleek dark coil of her scented hair, stimulating a shudder as she felt him bring it tumbling around her shoulders. Something seemed to be freed inside her at that moment and she gave a small cry deep in her throat as her senses abandoned themselves to the irresistible magic of his touch.

'Oh, Emma,' he intoned in a voice roughened by emotion. 'Why have we had to fight each other? I could be good to you. Let me. Let me be good.'

Her reply was stifled by the hot mouth that covered her own, his tongue questing inside her open lips, the whole masculine force of him pressing her into his arms so that she was beginning to feel there was no separation between the two of them.

When he released her she was in a daze. 'I offered to walk home with you,' he said in a voice that sounded drunk with some overwhelming force. 'Now I'm behaving like a street kid. What have you done to me?' He seemed to open himself for an instant before the baffled expression was replaced by the familiar poker face. 'Mark and Emma. Sounds good, huh?'

She was silent. There was nothing she could say that would adequately convey the wildness of her emotions. It was as if she had been swept by a tornado and set down in a strange land she had never guessed existed. Her secret self cried out for fear. He would annihilate her. Was this what it felt like? She was his creature, if only for a moment. Her body had tilted into his possession as abruptly as a suicide case might pitch herself over the edge of a cliff.

She forced herself to count the steps back along the pavement through the rain.

When she reached twenty she felt she had begun to regain possession of herself.

At thirty she managed to turn to him, extricating her arm from the one he had around hers, and at forty she said with a flippancy that should have earned her an Oscar as best actress, 'You certainly move fast, Mr del Sarto. Is this the usual way you do business?'

His step seemed to falter for a moment, either that or the pavement was uneven. Then the skin tightened across his cheekbones in a semblance of a smile. 'We're doing business, are we, Miss Shields?' His tone was level. 'I must say that's a novel idea. I hope it's going to be a mutually profitable arrangement.'

Emma glanced sideways at him. Were his eyes cold or merely guarded? she wondered. There was no way of judging. There was something chill in the atmosphere that hadn't been there before. Put another way, he was playing with her, and she had made an unexpected move. He didn't like it. That was what she was reading now from his guarded manner. But she had to defend herself against him because, for one wild moment out of time, she had been transported to some other place by an aberrant demon, and what she feared above everything was to find herself stranded there, alone.

'What you're asking yourself,' he said, still smiling, 'is this: is it lust, or something more?'

'I—hadn't thought of it quite like that,' she murmured in a faint voice.

'I had. Ever since last night.' His voice had roughened. 'I don't have casual relationships, but I'm not ready for anything heavy.' His eyes iced over. 'I don't know where that leaves us.'

'Nowhere, I guess.' She made an effort at lightness. Then honesty forced her to add, 'I don't want a relationship with anyone. I can't.'

'Can't?' He registered the word with a slight raising of his eyebrows. Turning, he ushered her forward, the umbrella held equally above their heads.

When they reached the gate of her house, she stopped abruptly behind the screening laurels. 'Thank you for seeing me home.'

'Is that it?'

'It?'

'Don't be obtuse.'

'I'm sorry.'

He nodded towards the house. 'Who is it in there?'

'No, I——' She looked down, confusion sending a bloom of embarrassment into her cheeks.

'If you're living with someone——' He reached out and gripped her arm. 'Well, are you?'

Miserably she stared past him into the rain. If she said yes, he would think the worst, but if she said no it would be a lie. Caught, she could only avoid his glance, letting it rest anywhere but on those piercing eyes.

His fingers tightened on her arm and she cried out with sudden hurt, her glance flying automatically to meet his, but he seemed oblivious to the pain he was causing, his face devoid of expression as his lips moved just enough to rephrase the question. 'How long have you been together?'

She shook her head. 'Please, let go of my arm. You're hurting me.'

He seemed to come to himself but without fully releasing her he allowed his fingers to course roughly down her arm to her wrist, convulsing for a moment, then reluctantly sliding away. 'So I take it you're not going to invite me inside,' he said tightly.

'I don't think that it would be a good idea,' she whispered, wondering why, what possible reason she had now to keep him at arm's length beyond the irrational one of fearing to be devoured by him in some strange way. The thought brought great waves of fear like the remembered fears of nightmare into her mind. They sent her swivelling away from him. 'I must go in.'

'He's waiting, is he?' The voice grated in her ear. 'Can't he wait to get his hands on you, Emma? Is that what it is?' His words raced on in a rapid undertone. 'Why can't you tell me about him? What sort of relationship is it? Why are you rushing back like this halfway through the afternoon? What is it that makes you so desperate to get back to him? What's he going to do to you if you don't go back? But you can't wait, can you? You're like a cat on hot bricks. You can scarcely bring yourself to talk to me, you're so possessed by the desire to get away from me to return to him. You even shut up shop an hour early to get back to him. I'm sorry I made the mistake of walking by. . . delaying you.'

She thought he was going to try to drag her away from the gate, to prevent her somehow from going inside the house, but when she jerked round and threw herself up the steps and turned to see if he was following, he was standing in the same spot, his face white in the gloom, mantled by the puma-black hair, lips taut with the urgency of desire.

'Go, then!' he snarled. One hand gestured as if dismissing her, and it was as final as if he was wiping her out of his life for good. She was shocked by the intensity of his expression. Did he always live life at this pitch of emotion? Yet his face seemed tight with the attempt to keep himself in check.

She stood in the porch at the top of the steps and stared back at him, unable to move either in or out. It was night now. She felt if she once went indoors he would go, leaving her forever.

'Mark!' she whispered. 'Mark. . .'

CHAPTER FOUR

EMMA raised one hand towards him and, as if it was some kind of secret sign between them and it drew him to her, he began to move slowly across the pavement to the house. In three strides he was at the top of the steps beside her. Neither of them spoke. Instead he crushed her against him, pressing her head into his shoulder while he smoothed her hair over and over with shaking fingers. When at last he raised her face to his she was trembling with the strain of keeping in check the warring of opposite emotions.

'This must be destiny,' he told her, his voice vibrating with the pent force of desire. 'What are we going to do, darling? I want to rush you away with me to some secret place where we can make love and forget the rest of the world forever.' A pulse quivered at the side of his mouth. 'Instead,' he rasped, voice suddenly coarsening, 'you have to leave me to go in there.' He nodded towards the house. 'Emma,' he tightened his grasp, 'you have to do something about this. I don't care if I'm pressuring you unfairly. I'll give you tonight. One night. Then you're coming to me.'

Her lips parted but she could find no words to convey how she felt. How could she explain in a few moments about Tom and what he meant? About her duty to him? About his dependence on her, and how guilty she would feel if she walked out on him? He had been right when he'd refused to take advantage of her compassion for him and marry her. He had known sooner than she had that it wasn't the sort of love on which a forever-after romance

59

was based. She supposed she had been too young, too inexperienced herself, to know that at the time. Yet how could she explain all this to a comparative stranger like Mark del Sarto?

And how, even after having explained all that, could she trust herself to a man who thrust such bewildering fantasies before her eyes?

He took her silence for agreement.

'Tomorrow,' he said huskily, 'we have tomorrow and all the days after that. He can have tonight and no more.' He bent his black head and devoured her lips in one burning swoop of passion, then released her as suddenly as he had taken her up, striding back towards the street before she could move. He slowed when he reached the gate and gave her a last lingering glance. 'Emma. . .' One hand was raised in a gesture that was a mix of warning, farewell and promise. Then he turned and was lost to sight.

Emma let out a sigh of breath—her limbs were trembling with the swiftness of what had happened. He seemed to have picked her up, spun her emotions in all directions, then set her down again, all in the space of a moment.

She turned to open the front door, but she couldn't get her key to fit in the lock and she had to pause, resting her head against the glass, then try again. This time she managed it, but even when the door swung open she could only hesitate on the threshold as if about to set foot in alien territory. What had he meant, she wondered frantically, what could he possibly have meant when he'd told her she had one night?

'Is that you, chicken?' Tom's voice rose pleasantly from the living-room.

'Just a moment,' she replied with a catch in her voice. She cleared her throat. What was she to tell Tom? That the enemy had colonised her heart, had practically seduced her on the doorstep just now? Shakily she hung up her coat and carried the shopping through into the kitchen to give herself time to think. When everything was properly stored away she put on the kettle and went through to greet Tom with a semblance of normality in her manner.

'Back early,' he observed, glancing up from the book he was reading. 'Had a quiet day?'

'Quiet?' Her voice seemed to rise out of control. It had been anything but quiet! But Tom didn't notice her agitation and she moved about the room for a moment, plumping up cushions and tidying away the morning's newspapers. He was an avid reader of news. She glanced tenderly across at him. How could she leave him when he needed her so?

He looked up and caught her glance. He was smiling. 'I've had a smashing day. Been out on the razzle.' He chuckled. 'Angelika took me for a spin in her car and we stopped off at a pub for lunch. She brought two ploughman's lunches and two ciders out and we sat in the car under some trees in the pouring rain. Paradise.'

'Angelika?'

'My physio, you remember? The new one. It was her day off.'

'Oh, yes.' Emma laughed. 'Silly of me. I hadn't registered her name properly. It was nice of her,' she added.

'She's a nice woman. I've already told you that. Lucky me, eh?'

'You're a flirt, Tom. I've always suspected it.' She was pleased he'd had a good day.

'I'm afraid I am rather,' he agreed equably. 'There'll be no holding me if I'm going into a period of remission.'

She lifted her head in surprise. 'Is that possible?'

He nodded. 'I've been feeling pretty good recently. Angelika says it's quite likely to happen like this.' He shut the book he was reading. 'I'll be able to help you in your fight against your property shark. We must get that settled before——' he frowned '—before I slip back.'

'Oh, Tom. . .' Emma leaned against the back of a chair. Should she tell him what had happened? What could she say? In reality nothing had changed. Her livelihood—and with it her ability to care for him—was still in jeopardy. No amount of stolen kisses and storm-grey eyes should blind her to the truth. The fight was still on.

She prepared supper later and they spent a cosy evening in front of the fire talking over the possible options open to them, how to mobilise the opposition, as Tom put it, and who to go to for help and advice. They drew up a short-list of people Tom would contact by telephone next day and by the time Emma got into bed that night Mark del Sarto's fevered embrace seemed like a figment of her own wild imaginings.

The man waiting in the car outside the shop, blatantly ignoring the double yellow lines and the traffic warden approaching along the pavement, was no fantasy figure, however. Emma spotted his silver Jensen from the end of the road and, although a voice warned her to turn and run, something else pulled her towards him as inexorably as the hand of fate.

When she drew level, at almost the same moment as the warden, she stopped. The passenger door swung open and he switched on the engine. She bent to peer in at him. 'Does that mean I'm supposed to get in?'

'If you're going anywhere with me, it does.' The hollows beneath his cheekbones deepened as he smiled across at her.

'You shouldn't be here. I think you're about to get a ticket.'

'Get in, then.'

'I don't think——' She shot a hasty look at the warden as he took out a little black book. 'Oh, all right, just for a minute, then I have to open the shop.'

She slid into the bucket seat beside him and before the warden could say anything Mark let the car out of gear and slid it smoothly into the stream of early morning traffic. There was a silkily romantic tape on the deck and Emma settled back with the intention of surrendering briefly to the sheer pleasure of being driven about by a handsome man in a car that epitomised luxury.

Luxury seemed to lap all around her and she stole a lingering glance at Mark as he concentrated on pushing the car through the traffic. He was looking gorgeous this morning, clean-cut features honed to an ascetic spareness, his sleek black hair immaculate, his lips firm and eminently desirable. He was in a grey suit again, a different one, the expensive tailored look enhancing the knotted muscles of his physique and almost asking her to reach out and run her fingers wickedly over his body. He gave her a brief, gleaming glance like an open invitation to do just that.

'The laconic Miss Shields. I can't tell you how I enjoy driving someone who doesn't try to distract me with a lot of chatter, especially at this time in the morning. Are you a morning person or a night person?'

'Night, I suppose. Maybe early evening.' She smiled, remembering the cosy evening she'd shared with Tom last night. 'What about you?'

'Definitely night.' He glanced sideways and she saw his eyes silver over her face before he turned back and gunned the car on to the ring road.

'Mark, where are we going?' she asked, suddenly

realising that he wasn't merely pulling round the corner out of range of the traffic warden but was in fact heading for a specific destination.

'Do you realise that's the first time you've called me by my first name?'

'Is it?' She knew it was and wondered what internal change had made his name slip so naturally from between her lips.

'You know it is.' He grinned. 'Truce, eh?'

'I don't know about that,' she replied lightly. 'Listen, where are we going?'

'Surprise.' He asked without expression, 'You've done as I wanted?' And when she didn't reply at once he went on, 'I mean, you've squared things with your partner?'

'With Tom, you mean?' The note of surprise was obvious.

'So it's Tom. I see.'

'What do you see, Mark?' Her head jerked to look at him. He was concentrating on the road ahead, calculating speed and distance with precision.

'Should we be doing ninety?' she asked.

'What did he say?'

'What about?'

'You mean you haven't told him about me?'

'I'm not sure what I was supposed to tell him.'

'So he's still living in a fool's paradise?' There was an edge to his voice. 'I asked you to tell him. I said one night. The rest of your time is mine.'

'I'm not sure I really understand. My time? My time's my own.'

'In the past, maybe. But you surely don't expect life to go on in the same old way, do you? Not now?'

Emma bit her lip and stared ahead at the fleeting countryside. When she spoke she was guarded. 'I don't know what you expect me to do. What has changed? What do you expect of me?'

'Expect or want?' He laughed mirthlessly. 'I'll tell you, Emma. I want us to play this thing out. I can't fight it. It may only be lust, but I think we're compelled to see it through.'

'I'm confused. I don't——'

'We're both confused. We need to spend some time together. Maybe then the confusion will sort itself into a beautiful pattern. Now I'm taking you back to the house I've just bought. I hadn't intended to live in it. It was for investment purposes. But I'm having second thoughts. I want to see what you think. Maybe you can advise me on how to furnish it? You obviously know something about period furniture. You might be able to advise me on the best places to get what I want.' He glanced in the rear-view mirror, then swung off the motorway on to a slip road.

In a few moments, while Emma was trying to sort out the jumble of thoughts his words had caused, he drove down a lane and eventually brought the car to a gliding halt on the gravel drive of a detached house set amid a small wood.

The garden was overgrown and the paintwork was somewhat faded, but the house itself was an attractive sprawl, windows jutting out at odd angles, charming crenellations above a round annexe and, the final touch, an elaborate conservatory at the back overlooking a tangle of lawn and flower-beds disappearing into a shrubbery.

'I like it,' she remarked as she climbed out of the car and breathed in the tang of grass and wet leaves. 'In fact, it's so beautiful it makes me want to cry!' Arms out-stretched, she spun round to face him. 'I adore it! You *must* live in it, Mark. It would be a crime to leave it empty!'

His expression didn't change. 'I never intended to leave it empty. I'd thought of furnishing it and doing company lets, something like that. I have plenty of foreign business contacts who would like somewhere to put their executives while they're doing business over here.'

'So it would not only appreciate in value over time, it would also bring you a monthly profit?' She couldn't help giving a nod of approval. He was a man she could understand.

They walked round the outside and after they'd inspected the gardens he took out a rusty-looking key and unlocked the front door. She stepped after him, footsteps echoing on the bare boards. After he had shown her round they finished up in the conservatory.

'Well, there it is.' He watched her face. Sunlight was filtering through the dusty glass and her hair gleamed like a dark halo in a shaft of light.

She moved out of the dazzle into the shadow. 'I suppose I'd better ask you to drive me back. I feel rather guilty at being so late getting into the shop.'

'Emma, you don't seem to understand. I'm offering you a commission. We'll talk figures when you've given me a rough outline of your plans. I think it would be best if you handled the furnishings as well. You can contract out for the actual making up.'

She looked at him in astonishment. 'You mean you're asking me to help you refurbish the place? But why? How do you know I could do it?'

He gave a short laugh. 'Don't you think you can?'

'You're holding something back.'

His eyes silvered with amusement. 'What makes you say that?'

'Intuition,' she shot back. 'You're far too shrewd a businessman to risk your hard-earned cash on an amateur. I could make an expensive botch of this whole place and land you in a lot of needless expense.'

'I know you could. But you won't. You're not an amateur.'

She lifted her head.

'Don't you think I've been checking up?'

'On me?'

He nodded.

A flicker of anger darted over her. 'Prying?'

'Don't start that.' He folded his arms across his chest and rocked back, watching her changing expressions with amusement. 'I've found a word for you.' His smile broadened. 'Want to know what it is?'

She pouted with annoyance. 'I really do have to get back. I'm losing business being here.' Was he serious about checking up on her? But how had he done it? She shuddered. She didn't understand the first thing about him.

Ignoring her he said, 'It's "malacostracan". How's that? Want to know what it means?'

She shut her eyes with annoyance.

'It means crustacean. I thought it summed up your Cancerian nature admirably. Crusty crustacean. Miss Crab. Listen!' He came over and took her swiftly by the wrist. 'We could be a great team. You don't seem to realise what I'm offering you. Do this place up, make a success of it, and we could be in business together. If it's anywhere near as good as I expect it'll lead to more commissions than you can handle.'

'But Mark——'

'Don't make excuses. It's the chance of a lifetime. I know you've got the right skills. I told you, I checked you out. You did a course at Christie's. You specialised

in art and antiques of the eighteenth century. That just
about covers anything I might be interested in. Now say
yes and stop playing hard to get. . .'

He was still holding her by both wrists. Without
trying to extricate herself she gazed at him in astonishment and asked, 'How did you know all that?'

He was looking pleased with himself. 'I had you
checked out by my people after the meeting the other
evening. It was merely to find out who I was up against,'
he admitted candidly. 'I'd no idea it would be of any
other use.'

'But you can't do that!' She was appalled. 'How could
you? How dare you?' Realising that he still held her
wrists, she snatched her hands away and stepped back.
'You mean to say you actually had professional snoopers
prying into my affairs?'

'Not your *affaires*, no, darling, that won't come till
later. But hopefully there won't be any.'

'What?'

He gave a mirthless laugh. 'You'll have to watch your
step. I can be very jealous.'

'Look, Mark, I don't think I understand all this.'

'Then let me explain,' he interrupted. 'I'm offering
you one very fat commission——'

'One step at a time.' She faltered. 'I haven't said I
want to take on anything else.'

'You're not stupid. Your bank manager thinks very
highly of you. You started up with a loan—he didn't say
where from, but I gather it was from a private source.
You've paid it back and now you're a financially viable
concern——'

'You mean my bank manager. . .? You've actually
been talking to him about me? But that's outrageous!'

'He happens to be keen for us to do business with
him, and when I asked one or two pointed questions he

very decently didn't contradict—we're talking big time, Emma. I don't think you've quite grasped who I am.'

'I don't care a damn who you are! It's outrageous to think. . . Does everything with you come down to doing business?'

'Now come on!' he laughed. 'With a birth sign like yours you surely don't object to that?'

'Leave my birth sign out of this!'

'Emma.' He was moving towards her, lips drawn back in a smile, but his eyes watchful. 'Am I going too fast for you?'

She dashed a hand across her forehead. 'It's like a nightmare.' What didn't he know?

The slate-grey eyes hovered above her for a moment before his arms slid round her waist, pulling her into an embrace which sent her thoughts spinning out of order at once. 'No,' she protested weakly as his lips hovered above her own. 'We must talk. . .' Then it was all liquid sweetness, a rapture of loving touch, a pulsing rhythm of desire as the world fell away.

'I had a crazy idea to bring you here and make love to you all day,' he groaned as his lips lifted for a moment, 'but I want it to be perfect the first time. I'm going to make it beautiful for you.' With a groan of regret he forced himself to hold her with less passion, and, one arm draped round her shoulders, he led her towards the main entrance. 'I've got to go out to the car to make a few calls. Have a look round while I'm gone and get a feel for the place. We'll come back to measure up near the end of the week. I want to get things moving as soon as possible.'

Without waiting for a reply, and with an impatience Emma was coming to expect, he went outside and she saw him get into the car and pick up a phone, dabbing in some information on to a portable database as he spoke.

Confused, she turned back into the house. Could he be serious about all this? She gazed up at the high ceiling of the main reception-room. It would look spectacular with a crystal chandelier in place, deep crimson carpets, something rich, a fabric perhaps, on the walls, and retexturing of the panelling which was rather dark and dulled by years of neglect.

Pulling herself up, she tried to consider the advisability of accepting the job, but all she could think of was the way he had taken her into his arms again. Was he serious about her too? But she couldn't allow that. It was simply monstrous the way he had pried into her private life, into her financial affairs—no one could forgive behaviour like that. So what was she doing now, trying to gloss over such an outrageous intrusion by dwelling on the way his lips had felt on hers. . .?

She was still undecided about accepting his commission or whether it would be best to storm out of his life there and then when he returned.

'It looks as if I'll have to get back to town. Something's turned up. I'll be away tomorrow, but maybe we can come up here the day after? And please, darling, don't worry. I'll slow down. Forgive me for rushing you. I'm a fool.' His glance was an enveloping caress, though he kept his distance. 'You'll look good here, Emma. It's a more appropriate setting than that little shop of yours. And as for that old house you're living in——'

He opened the door for her and stepped back as she walked through, but she was conscious of him following close behind as they crossed to the car. When they reached it he pulled her against him, pressing her back against the low-slung vehicle and giving her face a sombre examination. 'I know it's all very sudden, but I don't turn back once I've decided I want something.' He touched her face. 'You didn't tell me whether you'd had that talk with your—what is he? If not husband, what? Your lover, I suppose. . .'

'I suppose you've checked up on him too.' She ignored the word he'd used to describe poor Tom. Their relationship was nothing to do with him. He seemed to assume he had a right to pry into every little thing. She was still boiling over his gibe about her 'little house'.

His lips twisted as if her words caused him actual physical pain, but his eyes didn't lose their inscrutable calm. 'I always get what I want, Emma, and you may see me as one of the bad guys for taking somebody else's woman, but I can't help that. You're what I want. I must have always wanted you.' His eyes showed no evidence of any emotion but slid inch by inch over her face as if measuring her features for future reference. 'Don't tempt me to kiss you, otherwise I'll never stop and I don't want our first time to be on bare boards in a semi-derelict house. . .' His fingers pressured her spine. 'I'm going to give you the very best. Understand? Why don't you say something?'

Emma swallowed. Her voice was a croak when the words finally came out. 'Tom is very important to me. Nothing must hurt him. I've nothing else to say.'

Mark released her as slowly as if it was for the last time. 'OK,' he said expressionlessly. 'Let's go.'

They drove back to town in silence.

CHAPTER FIVE

EMMA felt her glance continually stray towards the shop window through which she could see pedestrians passing to and fro against a backdrop of town-going traffic. The quayside development which had brought Del Sarto Residential to the town was also bringing more traffic to the area.

When she caught herself gazing out of the window for the hundredth time that day she pulled herself up. All right, so Mark had dropped her off mid-morning with a curt, 'See you,' and before she could say anything the silver machine had inserted itself into the stream once more and disappeared down the road.

See you. It was a conventional farewell, if somewhat laconic. But it could mean anything. See you. . . some time if we happen to bump into each other. See you. . .but I don't know when. See you. . . as soon as ever I can get back to you.

She got up and rearranged some furniture, pretending to herself that she was getting things ready for the new pieces she had bought at a recent sale. They were due any day.

The thing was, she didn't want to see him. It was too dangerous. He was too fast, too passionate, too enigmatic for her. She didn't know where she was with him— whether the glimpses of passion he had allowed her to see were real or mere pretence. She frowned. What was this element of distrust she felt? Was it to be heeded, or did it simply mean she was scared of plunging too deeply into the hidden depths of her emotions? She longed to confide in someone for once, but it had never been her way. Tom was always telling her not to bottle things up, but she was only running true to type, wasn't she? How could she help it? She was the sign of the crab, scuttling for shelter when anything threatened her equilibrium.

The thing was, the uncertainty of wondering what he would do next was getting to her.

Then what she had been fearing and longing for all day suddenly happened.

He must have been standing looking in through the window for a full minute before she registered his presence. She felt a kick in her stomach and the breath was knocked out of her. Now, she warned herself. She bent her head and pretended to be going through the books.

The old-fashioned bell above the door jangled like an alarm of doom.

'Busy? Or can you finish for the day?' He was beside her, a living, breathing presence, full of life and danger.

She allowed herself a full second before she dared raise her glance. Slowly it travelled up the length of the powerful form standing beside her. He had on the slate-blue raincoat, unbuttoned as if he had come out in a tearing hurry, the sharp grey suit revealed in its opening, his strong face with its stormy grey eyes glowering down at her. But as their glances met he smiled. A dazzle of laser light, sweeping her up into his world again.

She felt her mouth open, lips part, pulses begin to race, as if, despite her best intentions, there was something inside her that couldn't help responding to him.

'Ready?' he murmured.

Her toes seemed to curl at the sound of his voice, a smoky invitation to unimagined sin. 'I'm busy,' she managed to croak. 'I really am.'

'Come on, you can't have had a better offer all day

than the one I gave you. If you have, name a figure and I'll double it.'

'Life isn't just a question of profit and loss,' she forced herself to counter. The words seemed to hang without meaning between them, while his glance devoured her. 'I mean, I have an obligation to my clients, my customers—I mean, go away, Mark. I need to finish. . .'

He placed his spread palm over the pages of the book lying on the desk. 'I told you last night to rearrange your life. If you haven't bothered to do so, too bad. Now you're coming with me.'

'See you—that's how you left me this morning,' she protested, unable to fathom what was happening. 'You didn't mention anything else.'

'But I'd already told you I'd be back for you.'

'Back?'

'Didn't I say I wouldn't be around tomorrow?'

She nodded, still not understanding.

'So, if I have to be away, I'm taking you with me.'

'But I have work to do——'

'There's a sale on in London. I expect to be able to buy something for the house. It's an important sale. You have the catalogue there, I see.' He gestured to a pile of brochures on her desk. 'You must know what's coming up. I need your advice. You can understand that. I might go mad and buy something totally worthless and pay over the odds. That's why I'm taking you on to my books, as adviser. I thought you understood.'

She opened her mouth and closed it again.

'We'll leave tonight so we can check into my club. The sale starts at ten. I don't want us to miss anything and it's best to avoid driving down in the morning. If we stay overnight we'll be nice and rested.'

'I——'

'So do you need to go home to pack a few things? We

won't do anything too splendid this evening. I thought a quiet meal somewhere and an hour or two to go over the catalogue together. All right?'

She closed her mouth and simply stared up at him.

'Emma, what's the matter?'

'I haven't quite taken in the speed at which you seem to operate.'

'You shouldn't be taken in by the unassuming manner.'

'Unassuming? You?'

'Sorry.' He didn't look it. He jerked his cuff and gave a glance at his watch. 'You're waiting for a client or something?'

As she slowly shook her head she knew she was sealing her fate. If it wasn't business that kept her here, he seemed to say, it could be thoroughly discounted. He went to the bentwood coatstand and took down her coat. 'You needn't worry about inviting me inside. I'll stay in the car.'

'Oh,' she said.

She felt his fingers graze her neck as the coat slid over her shoulders. Couldn't she say no? Couldn't she fight him? What on earth was wrong with her? Somehow words seemed to slip and slide away. He was already ushering her towards the door, efficiently switching off the lights as they went.

'Mark. . .' she began.

His face was ghostly in the sudden darkness of the shop. She put up a hand as if to ward him off, but he remained where he was, gazing at her impassively as if waiting for her to go on.

'Nothing,' she said.

He ushered her outside and, when she turned, fingers fumbling in her bag for her key, such a sense of unreality came over her that he had to take the key from out of her hand and turn it in the latch for her.

'There,' he said, 'that's that. Now let's go.'

She wondered if he had understood what she had tried to tell him that morning at the house. Tom was important to her. She couldn't just go off and leave him. His car was parked up the road, and when they were in it she ventured a word or two on the subject. 'It's Tom,' she began. 'I can't walk out on him——'

'It's all right,' he interrupted. 'I've already spoken to him. I rang up, pretending I thought you were home, and told him to remind you I'd be picking you up at six to drive to London.' He smiled with satisfaction. 'He obligingly told me that you were at the shop, but that he was sure you had everything under control.' He gave her a sideways glance. 'I found that remark rather puzzling. Unless it was a reference to your Cancerian practicality?'

She ignored the question in his voice.

'He didn't seem too upset that you wouldn't be showing up this evening—tonight, that is,' he added meaningfully.

'Why should he be? He trusts me,' she said shortly.

When she risked a glance at him Mark was smiling.

Sure that once she got inside the house she would be able to switch off the strange power he seemed to be exerting and resist him, Emma got out of the car as soon as it stopped. Without saying anything she fled up the steps and unlocked the door. Only when it was shut did she lean against it, her heart palpitating in a frightening manner.

'Emma?' Tom's voice called urgently to her and when she went through he was turned already to watch her come through the door. 'Did you see him?'

There was no need for explanation. 'He's outside now,' she said weakly, sinking down onto the sofa.

'Hurry then. I got Angelika to dig out the travel bag from under the stairs——'

'You what?'

Tom looked puzzled. 'I knew you were going to be in a hurry——'

'But Tom! It's *him*!'

'The shark. Yes. Well.' He paused. 'So what?'

'So *what*?'

'He seems to be offering quite a good proposition. He told me a little bit about it. You're not thinking of turning it down?'

'What did he say to you?'

Tom threw back his head. 'You're to do up a house of his. Wonderful! It couldn't have come at a better time. You're wasted in that little shop.'

'You must be joking!' She was genuinely astonished.

'But Emma, my sweet creature, what could be more useful? You do a job for him; he's honour-bound to help you when it comes to the shop. He won't have you bulldozed without offering something even better——'

'Are you *mad*, Tom? He's a predatory monster. I think his plan is to——' She bit her lip. 'I think he's just doing all this to get me on his side. I don't think he cares a damn about this house of his. He just wants me to be beholden to him in some way. . . I feel. . .' She swallowed back the words and looked at the carpet. Couldn't Tom see what was happening to her?

'Emma, sweetikins, he sounds as if he's really trying to do some sort of deal. Why are you being so funny about it?'

She raised her glance.

'Oh, I see. . .' He took in her stricken expression at once. 'This isn't like you. Normally so ice-cool.' He gave a soft chuckle. 'If it's any encouragement, your stars show a most fortunate phase for romance——'

'Tom, I don't know what's happening to me. I don't *want* a man like him. I can't understand what's going on. What does he want?'

'Ah. That's a good question. Apart from you, it's anybody's guess.'

'What do you mean, apart from *me*?' She stood up. 'I will not be a pawn in his game. He's too—he's too powerful. He doesn't live in our sort of world. We're the quill-pen brigade compared to him. He's all databases and car phones and jetting around from one merchant bank to the next. Have you seen his car?' She glanced towards the street. 'He drives a Jensen, for heaven's sake—and he puts it about as if it's an old Mini. Do you know how much they cost?'

'Quite a bit more than I managed to put into this pile of bricks and mortar,' Tom suggested, raising his eyebrows but obviously unimpressed.

'Tom, you are a child. Can't you see what he's up to?' Suddenly it was all beginning to make sense. She discounted the intense way he had looked into her eyes and concentrated on the facts. 'He knows I'm the central figure in the group who are working against him. He thinks by colonising me he can clip the wings of the whole group.'

'That's a mixed metaphor if ever I've heard one.'

'But see what I'm trying to *say*!' she almost shouted.

'I do, my love, I do. But couldn't you be wrong?'

She shook her head vigorously. 'How *can* I be?'

Tom grimaced. 'If you're thoroughly convinced, perhaps you'd better go along just to see what else he has up his sleeve? I've been on to your short list of possibles today and they've promised their full support. Anything you can glean—from the horse's mouth, as it were—would be most useful.'

'You mean spy on him?'

'I hadn't thought of it quite like that,' protested Tom, 'but if that's how you see it. . .'

'Oh, really, this is all too much.'

Tom gazed into the fire. 'Perhaps we're getting a little overheated about the problem,' he reasoned. 'Angelika's coming over later on. I'm going to talk it out with her. She'll put everything into perspective.'

Emma had a sudden feeling of superfluity. If Tom was beginning some sort of romantic friendship with his physiotherapist, she wouldn't stand in his way. She could see how he would want to make the most of his brief lease on life. . . Her heart turned over. Dear, darling Tom. She loved him so. And the feeling was nothing like what she felt for Mark del Sarto. It was the exact opposite.

There was an irritable toot on a car horn from outside.

'He's being very patient,' murmured Tom, giving her a glance.

'It looks as if my mind has been made up for me.' She turned to the door. 'Have a nice evening. I'd be interested to hear what Angelika has to say.'

She went up to her room and put a change of underclothes in the weekend bag that had been brought out for her. This Angelika was figuring rather prominently in Tom's life all of a sudden. She hoped he wouldn't get hurt. She had yet to meet her—what?—her rival? She shook her head. She and Tom had long since resigned themselves to being the brother and sister neither of them had had in real life.

Bag packed, she went downstairs again. 'I'll be on my way, then. We're supposed to be staying at his club in London. It sounds quite respectable. . .'

'I'm sure it is. He's a very single-minded sort of guy. My guess is, his mind will be on business tonight and nothing else.'

Emma nodded wanly. 'See you tomorrow when we get back then. What time is she arriving?'

Tom glanced at the clock. 'In half an hour. Don't worry. I'll be fine.'

She went over and placed a kiss on his forehead. 'Don't do anything I wouldn't do,' she told him automatically.

'Likewise,' he joked. He was already picking up a book as she let herself out.

Mark came round the car as soon as he saw her appear. 'That took some time. I thought I'd sorted him out this afternoon.'

'Yes, he said you'd called, but I wish you wouldn't talk about him like that.' She slid into the passenger seat and closed her eyes. Fate seemed to waft her onwards to some mysterious destiny whose outlines she could not yet discern.

They arrived in the West End at about seven o'clock and Mark drove them straight to his club just off a leafy London square where they checked into separate rooms and met a few minutes later in the bar. 'We could dine here,' he suggested. 'I feel like taking things easy this evening. I've quite a lot of paperwork to check out. You can go through the catalogue if you haven't already done so and mark anything you think would look right, then we'll cost it out and make a short-list.'

They did just that, making desultory conversation over a faultlessly served meal, and retiring to a comfortable sitting-room overlooking the garden shortly afterwards. Mark at once engrossed himself in a pile of

paperwork as he had told her he would and, armed with
the sale catalogue and a paper and pencil, Emma tried to
concentrate on the task he had given her. But her
thoughts were all askew.

With his head bent he seemed oblivious to her presence now, and she wondered just what was going on in
his mind apart from facts and figures. Why did he seem
to blow hot and cold? Now his feverish words outside
the house this morning seemed like a dream again, as far
removed from the ice-cool businessman who was sitting
in front of her as could be imagined.

He looked up and their glances meshed briefly. 'Well?'
He raised his eyebrows. 'Anything we should go after?'

She rifled the pages in confusion. 'Several things,' she
said, her mind a sudden blank. Fortunately she had
marked with a cross the things she thought might interest
him.

'Where do they come, at the beginning or what?'

'The dining table is lot three. That's the first.'

'We'd better make sure we're there on time.' He gave
her an enigmatic smile.

When he finished his work he came to sit beside her
and took the catalogue from between her fingers. Suddenly she was trembling at the sudden warmth of his
body against hers, but he appeared not to notice and she
managed to preserve a cool exterior despite the pounding
of her heart. 'Good,' he remarked after looking through
her list. 'All within the realms of possibility.'

'Pricewise, you mean?'

'These prices are only guesswork.' He indicated the
ones he'd pencilled in. 'I'm sure we'll be able to strike
lucky somewhere along the line.' He grinned. 'I like
sales. It's my gambler's instinct, I suppose. I like
winning, too.' His expression unfroze for a moment and
she saw the predatory gleam come into his eyes, but this

time she was relieved to note it was due to the prospect of the sale and not for anything more personal. At least she hoped not.

She began to relax a little. Nothing could happen that she couldn't handle. They had separate rooms, and it was such a very respectable establishment that she was sure there would be no tolerating any room-hopping, not even from respected members like Mark del Sarto. The uniformed men on Reception had done so much bowing and scraping when Mark appeared that she had felt she was walking into the past where masters and servants were divided by immovable social barriers, a world she had thought long gone. Mark, however, seemed not to notice. He was courteous to everyone in a distant, casual sort of way that brought the best from people, but never allowed them too close.

The way he is with me, she thought. Distant, yet somehow very present too. If I could talk to him, really talk, I wouldn't have this uncomfortable feeling that something I can't control is about to happen.

'Let's call it a day,' he said suddenly, slapping the pages together after skimming her final choice. 'Come on. One nightcap, then bed.'

She gave a little start but he seemed not to notice and pulled her up beside him, then walked on ahead to the cocktail bar. It was already nearly empty and he found a table for two in a corner and brought her a brandy and soda. 'We must do this more often,' he said, looking round. 'It's far more pleasant in here with you beside me.'

She gave a shaky laugh.

'Why do you smile?' he asked.

'Well, the idea's very nice, but it's not real life, is it?'

'How not?'

'I'm running a business. It doesn't allow for days off.'

He moved his head in a small nod of agreement. 'Maybe,' he said, 'we can find a way round that.'

'Mark. . .' She swallowed, wondering whether it was an opportune moment to broach the question of his plans just yet; then, irritated by her own reluctance to get things sorted out, she decided to plunge on. 'Are you still going on with your scheme—I mean, to pull down the block?'

He lifted his glass and drank, then replaced it, all the while giving nothing away by so much as a flicker of an eyelid until he said, 'What if I say yes?'

She was silent.

There was an uneasy moment when she thought they were going to have an argument, but he himself seemed to want to leave it there, and it was more than she could bring herself to do to persist in a discussion of it just now.

'Ready?' He rose to his feet without looking at her.

They went up together and when they arrived outside her bedroom door she turned, expecting him to say goodnight and walk on. His face was impassive as he took the heavy key on its ring from out of her hand and placed it in the lock. Assuming he was merely being polite, she allowed him to open the door for her and watched as he stretched inside and felt for the switch.

There were several wall-lights, giving a subdued glow, and it was a pretty room done out in peach and gold with a silky-looking bedspread on a double bed and floor-length curtains at the two windows. One of the maids had already drawn the curtains and turned back the bed and the room looked thoroughly inviting.

'Thank you for——' She faltered, giving him his cue to leave.

But he was shouldering his way in, already pushing the door shut behind him, and moving into the room after her as she hastily retreated, reaching out to take her into his arms. She was conscious of his hands coming round her waist, pulling her against him and effectively stopping her escape.

'Mark—I don't——'

'Emma, you do. You want me. . .' His lips softly plundered her own, moving rapidly over her face and mouth and into her hair, then back once more to the lips he was tasting like a gourmet. 'Have you worked out my sun sign yet, Emma?' he murmured as he teased her to a helpless response. 'It guarantees we're going to be dynamite together; all the signs say so. . . Come, let me undress you slowly. I want you to remember and relish every moment of this. . .'

'Mark,' she protested, 'please don't. I never thought you intended this tonight; I mean, I wouldn't have come with you—we can't! It's not right!'

'Right?' His eyes were bleared with incomprehension.

'I mean, I don't do this sort of thing.'

'What, never?'

'Not for a long time. . .'

'Then that makes two of us. . .' He was already unbuttoning her blouse.

'Please. . .' She clutched at his fingers and held them tightly between her two hands. 'I mean it. I thought you wanted me to help you choose furniture, not——'

'Not test it out?' He was laughing, not taking her protests seriously at all. He moved her backwards towards the bed. 'Let's test this fine example of twentieth-century bedroom furniture,' he murmured against her ear. 'What would you give for it? If it lives up to expectations perhaps we'll put in an offer for it, for sentimental reasons.'

'You're being difficult.' She tried to push him away. 'I mean it, Mark. I *don't want this*——'

Her words suddenly got through to him. He looked as if she had slapped his face.

But the familiar blank look at once obliterated his automatic response and she couldn't tell what was going on in his mind when he said, 'I warned you I was a night person. I couldn't sleep now if you paid me.' He let his hands trail from around her waist and stepped back. 'Let's have a drink sent up instead.' His mouth twisted.

Allowing his palms to smooth down her spine, once, with deliberation, eyes gauging her response as if cataloguing it for future reference, he said in a flat voice, 'Luckily, I have plenty of self-control.' She saw his eyes flicker once to the bed and the skin tightened across his nose and jaw.

She moved out of range and went to sit on a gilt chair near the window. He sat on the edge of the bed and picked up the internal phone. 'What would you like?' he asked her as he waited to be connected.

'Cocoa!' she said sharply.

His expression didn't alter. 'Two cocoas to room— what number are you?' He fumbled for the key and glanced at the disc. By the time he had replaced the receiver Emma was pacing the floor.

'What about the maid?' she demanded. 'You can't be seen here in my room.'

'Is that all that's bothering you? Convention? Typical Cancer!'

She shook her head, dark hair tumbling around her shoulders where his embrace had brought it down. 'You know that's not all,' she said in a small voice.

'You don't want me.' His face was like a mask and he didn't wait for her to either affirm or deny it. 'Plenty of time,' he went on. 'I can be patient. I don't mind playing cat and mouse if that's what you enjoy. I've already told you, I never lose control. . .' He paused. 'And I never lose.'

She was shuddering with a sense that one false move would send her pitching headlong over a cliff beyond which lay an endless drop into oblivion. 'We seem to have reached an impasse,' she observed. She felt close to breaking-point.

'Not at all. We're simply taking time out to prepare for the main game. Come and sit here.' He seemed entirely in control of himself when he patted a space beside him on the bed, and when she gave a vigorous shake of her head he grimaced and got to his feet, joining her on the window-seat where she was now perched so that when the maid brought their drinks on a silver tray they were sitting decorously at each end with a curve-legged coffee-table between them.

Emma noticed how his eyes followed the maid as she walked across the room. Admittedly she was pretty, and probably the high-necked black dress and white cuffs and apron appealed to something in his masculine imagination, but did he have to stare at her so deliberately? She was disgusted at the way his glance trailed over the girl's black stockings and, when she reached forward to place the tray between them, lingered beyond the bounds of politeness on the outline of her breasts through the black linen of her frock.

His face seemed to Emma to wear an expression of coarse sensuality. He knew she had seen it. She averted her head and pretended she hadn't.

When the girl had gone out he inclined his head to her, a smile playing around his lips, his cloud-grey eyes cataloguing her response. His expression was carefully blank. 'Let's talk,' he suggested. 'We've got all night.'

'Have we?' she said, voice high.

'I'm not going to be able to sleep. Are you?'

She averted her head in a gesture of disapproval.

'You're quite right about not wanting to go to bed just now,' he continued easily, as if it was a matter of supreme indifference one way or the other. 'It is too soon. Sometimes it's good to savour the pleasures ahead.'

He smiled without humour. 'We can pretend to be civilised about this, Emma. Why not? After all, we both know we'll eventually finish up as lovers, either here or somewhere else. . .' He gave her a predatory smile. 'It's as inevitable as sunset and moonrise.'

CHAPTER SIX

WHEN they had finished their drinks Emma really thought Mark would say goodnight and leave. But he didn't. And, contrary to what he himself had suggested, they didn't talk either. Instead he lapsed into a brooding silence. His strong, dark face expressed a kind of deliberate withdrawal that she found frightening. It was as if, despite his words, he could not forgive her for rejecting him. Now he was brooding over the punishment he would mete out. But, she thought fiercely, my behaviour has been blameless. If anyone has behaved badly, he has—inviting himself into my room, expecting me to leap into bed with him, ogling the maid in that grossly sensual way as if deliberately to demonstrate that there are plenty of other women available should he so wish. . .

'My sister,' he began suddenly, breaking into the maelstrom of her thoughts, 'was always heavily into astrology. It would be interesting to hear what she'd have had to say about this situation.' His eyes, cloud-grey, swept sightlessly over her face before returning to gaze into her eyes as if to prise a response from her. He got up and went to the intercom when it was obvious no comment was forthcoming.

Emma, still wishing he would leave, took the opportunity to go into the bathroom. Giving a sigh, she leaned against the cool marble above the washbasin, then took down a bottle of cologne and patted her temples with it. She was beginning to feel headachy and irritable. Why wouldn't he simply go away and leave her in peace?

88

Obviously her attitude had convinced him that there was no point in attempting a big seduction scene. And their conversation had somehow reduced itself to these truncated phrases and sullen looks. She felt affronted to the point where words were impossible. To think he seriously imagined she was likely to fall into bed with him, now or ever! He also probably imagined she was the type to betray her colleagues on the defence committee and tell him all their plans!

When he came off the intercom she was just returning from the bathroom and before she could say anything he rasped, 'Haven't we stonewalled long enough?'

'What do you mean?' She stood in the doorway, the cologne clinging about her in a scented cloud, with the throbbing at her temples as strong as ever.

'You're being deliberately quiet. Haven't you anything to say to me?'

'I rather thought it was the other way around.'

'I have plenty to say, Emma.'

'Then say it and get out.'

He rose slowly from the bed. There was something about the way he began to prowl forward that sent an icy trickle down her spine. She took a step back, grabbing for the bedroom door, her eyes widening as he stalked up on her.

His own grey eyes were riveted to her face and she heard herself babbling something about not meaning that quite the way it sounded, and then suddenly when he was nearly within touching distance he stopped, and his lips twisted into a mirthless smile.

'You're frightened of me?'

She shook her head violently, unable to account for the way she had involuntarily stepped back. Her pulses were hammering with the desire to run but, despite that, she knew there was something pinning her to the spot, forcing her to gaze up at him, powerless until she saw what he was going to do next.

'No,' he murmured eventually in a voice so quiet she could scarcely make out the words. 'You're not going to angle me into a corner like that. What happens is going to be the result of mutual choice.'

'What do you mean?' she managed to croak. 'I don't understand.'

'You're trying to make me take you against your will. . .why, Emma? Do you think it'll give you some sort of moral advantage?' He stretched forward to run his fingers down the side of her face and she felt herself thrill to his touch. 'No,' he went on, 'I don't play that sort of game. You'll want me, desire me, plead for me. And I'll wait as long as it takes to hear the words from your own lips.'

'I don't know what you mean. I'm not playing games with you—I don't know what you want. . .' she began in confusion.

His smile deepened, not quite reaching his eyes. It was just a tightening of the skin across his cheekbones, a drawing back of his sensual lips, nothing more.

Emma suddenly had a violent desire to see beyond the mask. She wanted to know why he was saying such things. Did he really believe she would plead to have him make love to her? What sort of man was he? Remembering his words just now, she longed to know what the 'plenty' was he had to say.

She edged along the wall until she felt the arm of a chair beneath her fingertips. Then she sank down and gave him a weighing glance from its relative safety. Her heart was thumping like a mad thing and she cast around for something neutral to say to take the steam out of the situation. 'Why do you talk about your sister in the past tense?' she asked, unsure why this particular question had leaped into her mind.

He gazed at her in astonishment for a moment. 'Because she is,' he said. 'Past. Dead.' He frowned and turned away. 'Car accident.' He swivelled back and gave her a piercing stare. 'If there was anything in astrology she would have known. But she didn't.' He moved away, and eventually went over to the other side of the room, picking up a magazine at random from the coffee-table then flinging it down without looking at it.

'I'm sorry,' she whispered.

'It doesn't matter.'

'I am sorry,' she said again, overcome by gentleness towards him. For once there was no attempt to disguise his feelings. They were plainly written on his face.

'None of us knows what the future holds,' he said abruptly. 'If we did. . .well, it's past now. It was a long time ago, but we were very close. It just happens I've been thinking a lot about her recently because of what she used to say about fate, the way it can link two people almost despite themselves. She also told me——' he gave a sardonic smile '—that I'd be happy with a woman born under the sign of Cancer. Of course,' he went on at once, the smile still riveted like a mask across his face, 'it doesn't mean it has to be you.'

He sprawled in one of the armchairs and gazed across the room at her, the shadow of his eyelashes making dark moons beneath his eyes. 'I'm beginning to realise that's most unlikely.' His eyes met hers. There was nothing in them. He went on, 'She used to say it was in my stars that I'd have an obsessive desire to possess what was out of reach. . .' He paused. 'That's why I'm such an innovative businessman.'

He opened his eyes and she could see straight into the grey depths, but even now, when he was talking in a

semi-confessional mood, they gave nothing away. He
said roughly, 'There are plenty of women in my life,
Emma. None of them out of reach. There's only ever
been you.'

'More fool them,' she said angrily. 'I will not be
picked up and used. I don't want casual affairs. I won't
have them.'

'No, you want a husband, a home and babies. I know
all that. I've read her notes for your sun sign. I've gone
back and read them again and again since I met you, as
if they can tell me something I don't already know.
There has to be something in there for us, something
that means something. . .'

'I just want to run my shop and look after Tom,' she
broke in, frightened by the intensity in his voice.

'Look after him?' The grey eyes flashed. 'Can't he do
that himself? What sort of man would want you to look
after him?' He gave a scathing laugh.

Emma couldn't answer. It would be wrong to offer
Tom's private life merely to have it picked over and held
up to scrutiny. Someone like Mark would be the last
man on earth to need anyone for anything, whatever
physical injury afflicted him. And sympathy for Tom
would be the last thing he could be expected to offer.

'So that explains a lot,' he ground out when she
couldn't speak. 'You're such a red-hot businesswoman
because you need to work to keep your layabout lover!'
Mark lifted his head and began to laugh without humour.
'That's marvellous. I really think that's wonderful. It's
the best joke I've heard in years. You really are the
sentimental type, fond of nursing sick animals! Is that
the way to make you want me? Would I stand a chance
if I was a loser? Is it failure that turns you on? Is that the
way into your bed, Emma?'

'I don't have to listen to this!' She was gazing at him

in astonishment. Did he know about Tom after all? If so, how could he possibly talk about him as a layabout and a sick animal? She shuddered. It was so cruel. But something else had stung her. 'Just for the record,' she gritted, 'you may as well understand that there's only one way into my bed, and it's obviously the route that has never occurred to a man like you! Now would you go, please? I'm tired. I want to sleep. We have nothing to offer each other. You're as hard as nails. I doubt whether you have a scrap of compassion in your entire body. You don't know what Tom's like, and if you really did even you couldn't say the sort of things you're saying. He's a good, kind man who deserves a better fate than the one he's got.'

'I'd be all sweetness and light too if I had you under my thumb,' he suddenly snarled. Rising, he came across to her and reached down before she could move to rive his hands through her hair, dragging her face up to his and forcing a kiss, a sensual raking of his lips over hers that was brief and powerful and left her breathless.

'See you in the morning at breakfast, darling,' he said with heavy irony on the last word. 'You've had a reprieve. I've told you what I'm going to hear from these lips——' He touched them with one finger, watching them tremble in anticipation, but then he stepped back and said, 'If the yearning in those expressive blue eyes of yours is anything to go by, I won't have long to wait.' His lips twisted for a moment before he swivelled and with an abrupt shrug walked to the door.

Emma watched him leave in utter astonishment. At first she felt cold. What on earth did he mean? Was he trying to say he took pleasure in seeing her so confused? And could he seriously imagine she was so bowled over by him that she actually wanted him to make love to her? He must be mad. He might make her feel some

wild reaction to his touch—she hadn't been able to
control the sudden upsurge of emotion at that raking of
his lips over hers—but it was due to surprise more than
anything else. Even he must realise that, if he gave it a
moment's thought. Her true feelings must surely be
obvious? They were pure dislike and anger, not what he
imagined at all.

And then to say he wouldn't have long to wait! The
arrogance of the man was stupefying. Her blood was
boiling. Tomorrow she would show him exactly how
long he'd have to wait—and it wouldn't be a day less
than forever! If he managed to extract a single glance
from her he would be a very lucky man indeed.

Brushing aside the fear his dark mood had aroused,
and concentrating only on his arrogance, Emma made
sure the door was locked then got undressed and ran a
hot shower, finally climbing into bed with the firm
intention of falling asleep at once. Instead she tossed and
turned for hours, first on one side, then on the other. All
she could think of were his soulless eyes boring into hers
and the assumption that he only had to wait long enough
for her to fall helplessly into his arms like an overripe
fruit. What had she done to make him think a thing like
that? Nothing. She seethed all night. Whatever had
happened between them had been his own fantasy. But
he'd miscalculated—she was a totally unwilling recipient
of his attentions. And he'd better believe it.

Despite her troubled night Emma awoke early and
decided to go down to breakfast at first call so that with
luck she would miss meeting Mark altogether. Then she
would only have the ordeal of sitting through the sale
with him before it was time to return to normality and
home.

But her plans were thwarted almost at once when,

letting herself out of her room, she walked slap into
Mark straight away. He was wearing a black jogging suit
and had a scarlet towel draped over his shoulders. His
hair, she noticed as he came down the corridor towards
her, was wet, gleaming like black leather, and then, as
he came even closer, she could smell the faint tang of
chlorine on it.

'You should have come for a swim with me,' he
remarked without any preliminaries. His glance raked
over her entire form with blatant provocation. She felt
stripped to the skin. Before she could counter it he said,
'You'd be a real turn-on in a sexy swimsuit.' He laughed
and walked off.

She watched him go, her thoughts, so carefully
arranged before she came out, thrown into a jumble of
incoherent longings and expectations. She felt winded.
He looked so wonderful. Tall, broad-shouldered, ex-
uding a masculine power that made nonsense of her self-
control.

But that look! Who did he think he was? For a
moment she saw red. Then she turned her anger on
herself.

What a fool she was! It was all right excusing herself
by saying that any woman would feel knocked out by a
man like him, but surely she could have more control
over her feelings than this? It was ridiculous. Even now,
moments later, her nerves were tingling with the sheer
firecracker power of his presence.

She shook herself, setting off for the breakfast-room
and making a list as she went. Surface good looks, yes,
that charisma or whatever you wanted to call it making
him blindingly attractive to the most exacting taste. But
that was the only plus as far as she could see. It was all
negatives after that—he was ruthless, dangerous and
arrogant. Impossibly arrogant, she reminded herself. As

well, he's insensitive—she frowned—possibly, but *certainly* bullying, totally self-centred and disgustingly obsessed with money, trampling on anybody and everybody to get more of the stuff. And he hasn't even got the manners to say good morning! she finished.

Having firmly settled things in her mind once more, she went into breakfast and was seated composedly at their table when he reappeared to chip at her shell again.

He gave her a grin as he drew back his chair, his manner easy and relaxed, but before sitting down he came round the table and leaned towards her. Before she could move he had given her a kiss on the side of the mouth. No sooner had she noted the gulp of yearning lodging itself somewhere behind her ribcage than he withdrew. He sat down and offered one of his unexpected, brilliant smiles, all silver and light and designed to be utterly heart-wrecking.

She glanced away. Armoured though she was, there were still shivers coursing hotly up and down her skin.

They breakfasted in silence, the rolls, the coffee, amid the discreet clink of silver and the contented murmur of the other diners. He had on a dark suit that had obviously been carefully built to enhance every line of his body, a plain white shirt, and a deep red tie to contrast with his panther-black hair. Hair, she thought dreamily before she could stop herself, that reminded her of forests at night, and, with a *frisson*, the predatory creatures lurking in it. And when for one guarded moment his grey eyes dwelt on her lips, they seemed to lighten almost imperceptibly, shooting flares of silver in her direction that went straight to her heart.

'You look terrific,' he murmured. 'Blue suits you.' When their eyes meshed again her hand jerked and she nearly spilled her coffee. 'You're chic and glossy like a

movie star, lacquered and super-real,' he said. He leaned
back to give her an examining glance. 'Did you sleep?'

'Brilliantly,' she lied, avoiding his eye.

'I'm surprised you slept at all after what went on. I
didn't mean to put you through it like that. I'm a touchy
devil.'

She bit her lip to quell the instant retort and tried not
to succumb to this new, gentler version of Mark del
Sarto. It was only a ploy. She wasn't stupid. He was
trying to get round her.

He went on in something more like the old vein when
he smiled and said, 'We must make it a rule never to be
alone in a room with a bed in it. Not unless,' he added
meaningfully, 'we intend to lie on it.'

'There's not much likelihood of that,' she told him
tartly. 'On' it, he had said, not 'in' it. There was a subtle
difference. She made a mental note to remind herself of
that point at regular intervals. Already her resolution to
remain aloof from him was cracking. Gone this morning
was his dark mood of the previous night. Instead he was
charming and charismatic, almost as if he knew she had
been planning to remain aloof and had made up his mind
to best her by sheer niceness.

Very shortly they set off for the sale-room in Kensington
and arrived in good time, sitting together at the front
with Emma ticking off the lots as they came up and
Mark doing the bidding. Needless to say, he got everything he wanted.

He turned to her with a satisfied smile when they'd
finished. 'Things have certainly gone our way this
morning.'

As they came outside and looked around for somewhere to have a drink before driving back, she felt his
hand in the small of her back. People turned to look at

them, obviously recognising Mark, and she felt a strange
feeling of power as it cloaked her too. His presence was
acknowledged by everyone who looked at them, and it
gave her an odd jolt to see it. It told her what she knew
already: he was a man to be reckoned with.

He was smiling as he guided her towards a small bar
on a corner of the street. 'Let's have a quick bite then
get going.' He looked down at her. 'We do make a good
team, Emma. You know it. We could be devastating
together.'

There was much on Emma's mind while they drove back
towards home. Mark seemed now to be putting himself
out to be pleasant. But she couldn't understand why. He
was a man who would always have a purpose, she told
herself, so where was the purpose in being nice to her
now?

When they drew up outside the shop he let her get out
without making any reference to another meeting. She
waited, expecting some suggestion for getting together
maybe later that evening, and wondering what he would
say when she refused, but no invitation was forthcoming.
In fact, he seemed impatient to be gone and hadn't even
switched off the engine.

She hesitated, her hand on the passenger door. It had
suddenly become so pleasant to be with him that she
didn't want to let him go. When he still didn't make a
move to arrange anything, she let the door swing shut.
Then she bent down to say goodbye and saw him raise
one hand. There was a distant smile on his lips and he
seemed to be thinking of other things already.

She turned as he drove off, determined not to let him
see her watching him, but by the time she reached the
door of the shop she couldn't restrain a single glance

over her shoulder. He was a distant blur in the flow of traffic.

It was cold and dark when she opened the shop door and made her way towards her office. The aisle between the ranks of furniture was narrow. There was a smell of dust and lavender wax. Her reflection came back dimly from the old mirrors lining the walls. They showed a pale face framed by shining dark hair, full, rather determined lips, and eyes that he had said looked yearning.

She peered into one of the mirrors, studying them for a moment, then turned to her office with a gesture of impatience. She was mad to give him another thought. After all, wasn't that what he wanted? He would delight in the fact that she had been nonplussed by his curt goodbye and was wasting time now thinking about him.

It was good to be back at work. It felt as if she had been away for ages and she settled in with a will, clearing the morning's neglected correspondence and getting things back to normal. She enjoyed the security of having her own place with all her own things gathered around her. She had already given Tom a ring from the hotel that morning, but now she rang him again just to make sure he was all right and, in some odd sort of way, to reassure herself that her world remained the same after the devastations Mark del Sarto had wrought under the surface.

Tom picked up her call at once. There was the sound of music in the background and a female voice that stopped as soon as he started to speak.

'Love—nice of you to call. We were just off out.'

'You and Angelika?'

He chuckled. 'How did you guess?'

'I won't keep you, then.' They exchanged a few more

comments before phoning off. Emma was swept by an
unaccustomed feeling of emptiness after she put the
receiver down. Of course she was glad Tom was so
happy. But it disturbed the pattern of the last few years
to find that it was he who was branching out, for she was
used to the idea that that was her prerogative.

Sighing, she retidied her desk and checked over a few
invoices, and soon her misgivings were forgotten in the
usual comforting routine. There were quite a lot of
customers and she left finally at six o'clock feeling rather
pleased with herself and with life in general. On top of
that there was an irrational feeling of anticipation as she
let herself out into the street.

Her glance swept the roadside at once.

Instead of the comfortable feeling continuing, she
experienced an abrupt sense of loss. It was empty.

It wasn't that she actively wanted to see him. But the
fact that he wasn't waiting made an immediate impact.
Her spirits went into a spiral dive.

Pulling herself up sharply, she snapped the door shut,
and without allowing herself even one more glance up
the road set off on the short walk home. It's good, she
told herself fiercely as she went down the street. I didn't
want to see him anyway. He's the last man on earth I
wanted to see. I just thought. . .was worried that. . .let's
hope that's the last I'll see of him!

Contrarily, the thought didn't bring back the comfortable feelings she had been experiencing throughout the
afternoon. Somehow they had evaporated. It was a slap
in the face that he had chosen to keep away. As if a
promise had been made and had now been reneged on.
Yet he hadn't promised anything. And, after she had
rejected him, how could she expect him to want to keep
things going?

To make matters worse, Tom was still out when she

got back. There was a note lying on the kitchen table in an unfamiliar hand. It said he would be eating over at Angelika's and for her not to worry.

Good, she thought, taking off her coat and bustling about the kitchen. She reminded herself that she was pleased with the way things were turning out, and, later on, hunched over a hurriedly concocted meal made up of spaghetti and whatever else she could muster from the fridge, she sat in front of the television watching the nine o'clock news in the empty house and told herself once more that she was delighted with the way things were turning out.

Tom had still not appeared when the next programme finished. She told herself she would have to learn to let him go. As he had sometimes reminded her, it was no good hanging on to the past.

As if unable to follow this advice, she thumbed through a photograph album later on, fingering the pages with a nostalgic expression at the sight of Tom and herself in the early days of their relationship. Six years ago she had been a child, she realised, looking at the smiling young girl with a sense of loss. That innocence, that optimism, she thought. It was difficult to believe how naïve she had been in those days. She warned herself to be grown-up now about Mark del Sarto. Six years on from now she would no doubt feel the same way—if there were any photographs to record how stupid she was being.

As she got ready for bed she told herself she was sad only because she was unused to being left behind while Tom went gallivanting. But she was honest enough with herself to know it was a lie.

In a way she dared not examine too closely, her feelings had somehow been engaged by Mark during their sojourn in London—and now she was suffering the inevitable hurt. That was the trouble with poking one's head out of the shell, she observed, remembering a phrase from one of Tom's astrology books. Cancer woman, hiding inside her shell. So be it. It just happened to be the safest place with men like Mark del Sarto on the prowl. Shells were a protection against predators. She had been rash and foolish to poke even a fingertip into view.

Crabs had no need to fear the outside world because they always had a shelter to protect them. Emma's shelter was her shop and her home and her sound common sense. Mark del Sarto might threaten the security of her shop, but he couldn't put her out of business, he couldn't threaten her home, and, as for her common sense, it was as solid as ever.

Almost a week passed before she saw him again. By that time her defences were more firmly erected than before, and she scarcely faltered when she saw his sports car lying in wait for her outside the shop.

'You're an early riser,' she remarked as he uncoiled from within at the sight of her.

He loped over the pavement towards her. 'Wrong,' he announced, matching her tone. 'I've been up all night.' He smiled with a sharklike satisfaction but gave no further explanation.

Seeing at once that there was something on his mind, she turned and made abruptly for the shop, to get away from him suddenly her only desire. But he matched her speed and they arrived at the entrance together. He put a hand over the doorframe, barring the way. 'Well,' he demanded. 'I hear you've been up to a few little games while I've been away.'

'Away?' she exclaimed, then, focusing properly, corrected, 'I don't know what you mean by games.'

'You know what I mean, Emma, don't try to pretend. Fancied seeing your name in print, I suppose?'

His eyes were like two steel blades and she flinched as they bored into hers. She couldn't restrain a shuddering breath. What she was seeing was naked rage lashed down into a semblance of control. And he had the distinct aura of a man on the verge of letting go completely. As carefully as she could she said, 'I suppose you're referring to the piece in the paper the other evening?' It had been a good piece, giving their side of the current controversy over the development plans. She had been pleased with it.

'My Press secretary sent it on to me,' he intoned flatly. He seemed to move closer.

'Let me go,' she muttered. 'I'm late and I've got some phone calls to make.'

'Were you behind it?' he asked, still carefully casual.

'Yes,' she admitted, remembering her suggestion to Tom that the protest group should get in touch with the Press. It had been Tom who had got the whole thing moving, though. She tried to insert her key in the lock but he pushed it out of the way. 'Why, Emma?'

'Why what?'

He gripped her wrist, 'Why say all those things, trying to make me out to be some heartless blood-sucking monster whose only interest is trampling the little people into the dust?'

'Aren't you?' Suddenly she felt her blood boil, almost a week's uncertainty about her feelings for him pushing to the surface in a sudden eruption. 'You care only about one thing, Mr del Sarto, and that's Self. It matters not a jot to you that you're destroying the livelihoods of half a dozen people, some with families—and dependants,' she added, remembering Tom, 'and all because you want to make a few more millions to add to the millions you

already have. Well, it's not on! We said we'd fight. And
we shall.'

His face had assumed its habitual masklike com-
posure. He looked like ice. 'I see,' was all he said.

He moved away from the door and she quickly
inserted the key and opened it. She had just got inside
and was beginning to feel a flicker of relief that she'd
escaped unharmed when she felt a hand slam the door
back and he crowded in behind her. There was a click as
he jerked the door off the latch. At once she was a
prisoner in her own shop.

He was following right behind her and she could feel
the sudden heated energy of him as he came closer still.
'All right,' he ground out, 'if that's the way you see it,
let's have a review of the ground rules, shall we?'

Emma spun to face him. 'What ground rules? I wasn't
aware you played to any rules whatsoever?'

They glared at one another, neither one willing to give
an inch. He told her, 'I've played along with you so far
because of my better nature——' and at her explosive
laugh went on '—but, if you don't see that, it's a waste
of time explaining. I may as well go all-out to get what I
want.'

She was so shocked by the snarl in his voice and the
eruption of what looked like genuine emotion on his
impassive features that she could only stare at him.

'Get this, Miss Shields,' he went on when she didn't
speak. 'If you publish any more of this defamatory
rubbish, you'll be in a court of law before your feet have
time to touch the ground. I will not have my company's
name dragged through the mire——'

'Oh, that's rich!' she exclaimed. 'What have we said
that isn't true?' She gazed at him in blank amazement.
'You can't sue us for telling the truth.'

'Truth, dear innocent, is like beauty.' He drew his

lips back in a grimace halfway between a sneer and a
snarl. 'It exists entirely in the eye of the beholder.'

'In that case,' she came back at once, 'our idea of truth
is as good as yours!'

'Not so fast. I haven't finished. You, for
instance——' he put two fingers under her chin and
tilted her face up '——might seem like a hard-boiled,
calculating bitch to some, while to others you're a sweet
innocent who floats happily through life without a
scheme in her head.' He gave a mirthless laugh and let
her chin drop. 'It just happens,' he went on, voice heavy
with irony, 'that things fall your way—like this——' He
tapped the side of an inlaid cupboard that, it was true,
she had acquired for next to nothing because the old lady
who had asked her to value it, had said she reminded her
of her daughter when she was twenty-five. . .

She blushed, wishing she hadn't told him the story
after all on that first night in the restaurant. 'But you
can't sue us,' she repeated, shaking off the doubts his
implacable manner had aroused. 'How can we be held
responsible for what the local Press say about you?'

He gave her a vicious glance. 'I'm not going to argue
with you. We could stand here forever discussing it. You
won't see reason. So let's not waste time. Just get this.
Let this sort of thing happen again——' he tapped the
Press cutting in his hand '—*cause* it to happen, in any
way be involved in its happening, and then sit back and
contemplate the next stage. Because believe me, darling,
you won't find it at all pleasant.' He glanced briefly
round the shop. 'I'm sure you'd hate to lose all this—
and the house,' he added, 'with all its contents.'

'But that's a threat, Mr del Sarto, and when my living
is at stake I don't frighten easily.'

He gave her a glance like flint and she saw his lips
tighten. Despite the lack of expression in his eyes the

effect was similar to gazing across an ice-waste. It chilled her to the marrow.

'You made the first strike in this war,' he grated, 'and I've held my hand till now—but whether I retaliate or not is up to you. Just remember, in a war of attrition, you and your friends don't stand a chance.'

There was nothing she could say in reply. If she argued their case it would make matters worse. If she stood up to him and fought it out it would be worse still. And if she tried to switch on the charm he would view it with scorn. Silence seemed the only course.

He gave her one burning glance after he finished speaking, then slowly backed towards the door. The bantering tone of his farewell would have fooled a casual observer, but Emma was not taken in. He had meant every word just now. He exposed her to a final raking glance, then raised a hand and was gone.

She swivelled into her office. He was vile. He was the most vile man she had ever met. Why did they have to cross swords like this? She felt mauled and humiliated. There was no doubting that he would do what he said he would. A sudden tide of tears welled up, spilling out of her eyes and down her cheeks in a helpless flood.

He hated her. He really did. Only a man who hated could make threats like that. She had been right all along to suspect he'd been using her all those times he had switched on the charm and made her think. . . She cut off the memory of what it was he had made her think, ground her teeth into her lower lip and instead asked herself if she had ever seen any real warmth or kindliness in the arctic expression on his face. No, never, she answered her own question. He had always looked impassive, emotionless, as soulless as a snake. He was as indifferent to her as if she were a mere piece of furniture in the shop.

The tears scorched her cheeks, drying almost at once in their own heat. It was her life he was threatening. And he didn't care a damn. It was beyond belief to remember that she had almost fallen for that faint air of sympathy he'd adopted. He had almost seemed to understand her point of view. And his attraction towards her had seemed genuine too. Now she knew the sympathy had been a pose and the attraction only lust—an obsession, as he put it, for what was out of reach. Now she felt as if she were faced by a wall of granite and it was moving inexorably forward, crushing everything within its path.

With a sob she covered her face with both hands, shoulders shaking, tears streaming from between her fingers, crying with an abandon she would only ever show in private.

Still in her coat, she was like this when the jangle of the Victorian bell above the door warned her that someone had come in. Before she had time to scrub away the tears, a dark shape charged towards her down the shop.

'Emma!' It was Mark.

He came to a stop in the doorway of the office. Whatever he was going to say froze on his lips when he saw her face. His dark brows, furrowed by anger, lifted with the faintest trace of surprise. 'Emma?' he said in a different tone. 'You're crying. . .'

CHAPTER SEVEN

THERE was a long silence while Mark stood in the doorway peering down at her, an expression of total mystification on his face. Before he could speak Emma got up, dashing her hands over her eyes and giving him a hard stare.

'Don't you ever think twice about barging on to other people's property? I know you own all this, technically speaking, but there are limits!'

'Oh,' was all he said, the look of mystification still evident.

Through her rapidly drying tears, she went on, 'At least have the tact to go away until I've pulled myself together.'

'Is it——?' He didn't move and the look was still there. 'Is it something to do with——' he frowned '—well, damn it—with me? With what I've just been saying?'

She gave him a withering glance. This was where she had to act to save her life. 'You're so utterly conceited!' she exclaimed witheringly. 'That's exactly the sort of assumption I'd expect an arrogant devil like you to make. No, Mr del Sarto, my tears are not for you, as it happens, nor could you ever do or say anything to bring me to this state of sorrow.' She paused and half turned. It was a ploy to avert her head.

'Go on,' he growled from close behind her.

'It's a quite different matter,' she managed to say, the sudden huskiness in her voice adding the final note of conviction—she was amazed at herself: she could convince him—almost convince herself even—that he had no effect on her.

'Has something——?' He paused again, uncertainty having replaced the mystification on his face. 'I mean, has something else happened?' He shrugged, eyes never leaving her face.

'So it would seem.' She smiled sweetly, the tears still embarrassingly wet on her cheeks. Then she dashed them away with the backs of both hands. 'It's a personal matter,' she clipped, moving abruptly to the door as if to bar the way to her inner sanctum. 'I'm sure you didn't come back to discuss my personal affairs, Mr del Sarto. Now, is there anything I can do?'

He blinked and stepped back as she politely but firmly edged him out into the shop. 'I forgot to mention the house,' he said abstractedly. 'We need to get together to discuss the next stage.'

'The house?' She frowned.

'Larwood Hall,' he prompted without changing his expression.

In all the confusion of the last week, when he had apparently disappeared from her life forever, she had almost forgotten that they were supposed to be working together on the refurbishment of it. Now she thought quickly. 'There's too much uncertainty over the future of my business,' she said with a distant smile. 'I'm sure you understand. And I do feel it would be best if I passed up the opportunity of working with you. My security lies with the shop, not with one-off commissions like yours.'

His eyes were like slate. 'You mean you're turning me down?'

'You, Mr del Sarto?' She forced a vague, puzzled look

on to her features. 'I'm turning down your commission,' she clipped. 'What else?'

'You're turning me down, Emma, and you know it. Stop this fooling about.' He peered into her face as if he couldn't quite believe what he saw there.

'I'm sorry,' she replied smoothly. 'Have I missed something somewhere along the line? You're not seriously thinking we could work together after this morning, are you? As for any other sort of connection. . .well, really!' She gazed distantly into his eyes, holding his glance until for once he was the first to break away.

He turned and took a pace down the shop, then swivelled to confront her. 'When's that damned table going to be delivered to my apartment?' His uncertainty seemed to have vanished and he was in business mode again.

'I'm sorry. I thought they had delivered it.' She drew in a breath, relief flooding through her at having an excuse to drag herself out of his orbit—he was still looking at her as if he could laser straight into her mind—and she went into her office and pulled down the order book, flicking it open and glad when it fell instantly open at the right place. Even Mark del Sarto must be impressed by her efficiency, and a tiny victory, even one hardly worth noting, was important right now. She needed everything she could to shore up the breach in her defences. She might look and sound as if she was in control, but inside. . .

He was back in the doorway.

'Yes,' she announced, raising her glance and giving him that faraway look once more. 'It was delivered last Thursday. As——' she paused '——I said it would be.'

'I haven't been back to the place yet.' He didn't call it home, she noticed. Now he was looking confused again, whether by her efficiency or her manner, or by something to do with the tears he had surprised, she couldn't tell.

He went on standing in the doorway even when she closed the book and placed it back on its shelf. 'Well?' she asked coolly. 'Anything else?'

His eyes were like stones. 'Is that supposed to be your last word on the house issue?'

She nodded. 'I think it would be for the best, don't you?'

'I thought you Cancerians were supposed to like all that sort of thing: interior décor, turning houses into homes?'

'In my experience it's the people in a house who turn it into a home. Not the lavishness of the furnishings.'

Mark's face bore no expression whatsoever. 'You can let it go after all the trouble of helping me choose the furniture?'

'If I hadn't done it someone else would.'

His head jerked as if a blow had been aimed at it. 'Sure,' he said roughly. 'Someone else.' His face had a sudden pallor. A trick of the light, she thought, trying not to let her glance stay too avidly fastened on his features. How she longed to hold him, to feel his lips ravage hers in that possessive, strangely protective way. She shook her head to clear it. 'Is that all?'

He looked round the small neat office, letting his glance dwell on the blue vase with the yellow flowers in it, the neat shelves of reference books, the arrangement of shells on her smart rosewood desk, taking in the pictures on the wall and the pretty bits and pieces left over from the shop—as if making an inventory.

'I think I'll give you a day or two to think it over,' he said at last. 'It's no good being rash about something like this. After you've given it some thought you may change your mind again.'

'You make it sound as if you believe I'm acting on a whim, but I can assure you when it comes to business I do know my own mind.'

'I'm sure you do, Miss Shields,' he said, heavily sarcastic. 'As I said earlier, beauty and truth are purely relative.'

She understood at once what he meant. He was referring to his comment about how hard-boiled she was, and to all the rest of that scalding tribute. She felt a blush of anger dry the last of her tears. 'Are you likely to do me the favour of leaving now?' she bit out.

He shrugged. 'I guess you still have that right—to throw me off the premises, I mean. But make the most of it. It may not last. And Emma——' He paused, half turning to go, his lips, she noticed, compressed in an unforgiving line. 'Your tears were very touching. It shows that even a woman like you can be moved. Or has your lover run off with some priceless possession?'

'Get out,' she whipped back as soon as his words had sunk in.

'Do you still think he was worth it?' He gave her a drawn-out look, adding, 'Maybe you'll be more careful who you shack up with next time.' With a look of something she took to be contempt, he ducked his head and went out.

Rage and a sudden wild, irrational spasm sent her out of her chair to the door. He was already halfway down the shop when she called out, jerking him to a halt.

'If you're referring to Tom, you're talking utter clap-trap, Mr del Sarto! He's worth a million of you with your nasty calculating mind and I don't regret a single minute of the time I've spent with him. Now get out of my shop, you rat, and don't dare set foot in here again until I tell you!'

He turned slowly like a man roped. 'I've got all that, Emma. Every last word. And I should warn you,' he sighed, 'I have a very, very long memory.'

'Me too,' she spat.

'Good. I'm pleased to hear it. I guess that means you're not going to retract?' He paused, one look at the determined set of her chin telling him all he needed to know. 'In some ways we're evenly matched.' He gave her a lazy smile. 'But I guess I have the edge. . . Till the next round, then. So be it.'

Emma was trembling so violently after he left that she had to go and sit down, and she didn't hear the shop bell ring and was therefore surprised when a customer appeared in the doorway. Soon the day was in full swing and she found herself going through the motions: buying, selling, swapping jokes, efficiently running through her paces without a crack in the façade, while all the time beneath the surface she was in the lower echelons of hell.

That evening, while she was toasting some crumpets in the fire just before bedtime, Tom gave her a worried glance. 'Things have happened rather quickly between Angelika and me,' he began. 'The last thing I want to do is hurt you, Emma. . .'

'Tom——' she reached for his hand '—I'm so pleased for you both. You're a new man. She's obviously good for you. Don't worry about me. If I seem preoccupied this evening it's because I'm fretting over the shop.' In fact it was true. She felt numbed, like an accident victim suffering from shock. She went on, 'I don't think we're going to get the better of del Sarto——' she said his name as if it meant nothing '—and I think I ought to start looking for somewhere else. The problem is where, and as usual it comes down to money. Premises in town are really beyond our means. I simply don't know which way to turn.'

'It won't come to that. I was talking to a friend on the council only yesterday. He told me the planning committee haven't got all the details in from del Sarto's side and therefore they can't consider his application to have the place pulled down until the next planning meeting. They're obviously not as efficient as he'd have us believe. Either that or they're deliberately dragging their feet for some obscure reason of their own.'

'So they'll miss the deadline to get their application in?'

'Yes, and the one after this one isn't for another three months. It means you've got a reprieve, at least.'

'Reprieve?' The context for Mark's use of the word came back. It had been that night in her room at his club. Reprieve in that context meant withdrawal, neglect, indifference, a turning of his attentions elsewhere perhaps.

'What's the matter? You're not quite here tonight.' Tom peered into her face. 'You do look done in, love. There's nothing else, is there?'

She shook her head. Now Tom was involved with someone else she felt she hadn't the right to burden him with the stupid details of her personal life. Anyway, what on earth was there to tell him?

'You shouldn't bottle things up. You Cancerians are all alike.' He tapped her on the shoulder. 'Come on, snap out of it.'

'You know I can't.' She gave a rueful shrug. 'There's no point in being all emotional and whining on about things. I'm all right. I just feel threatened. It'll pass.'

'Hmm—will it?' Tom looked thoughtful. 'If it's anything you want me to know, you only have to come to your old Uncle Tom, you know that.'

'I do,' she whispered. 'I do know, Tom. You're sweet. And I'm all right, really.'

They sat for another half-hour without saying much, then she helped him out of his wheelchair on to the bed in the front room, finally going upstairs to her own room and lying down on the coverlet for a few moments, feeling somehow drained of the energy required to get undressed. Finally she forced herself to slip into her nightclothes. There was such a sense of doom about the whole situation that she found it impossible to separate her thoughts from the gloomy swirling of her feelings, but for the moment there was nothing she could do about it.

Mark wasn't the sort of man not to keep his word. And he had promised some sort of comeback. All she could do was wait.

She did not have to wait long. The form of his retaliation arrived a few days later in the shape of a long brown envelope bearing the del Sarto logo, a shield shape with his three initials entwined in it. With trembling fingers she ripped it open, rapidly read the contents of the letter inside, then clenched her teeth. The bastard, she muttered beneath her breath. He can't do this.

When she had got over her initial shock she went next door to see Jenni. She held out the letter. 'Did you get one of these?'

The look of mystification on Jenni's face was only allayed after she read the contents. 'You mean he's going to triple your rent and change the terms of your lease from next month? But he can't, can he?'

'He can,' said Emma in a flat voice. 'My lease comes

up for annual review next month. He can do just what the hell he likes.' She smiled grimly. 'I gather you haven't had one of these, then?'

Jenni shook her head. 'I've just had the usual renewal. I'm on a short lease anyway. But, Emma, I don't pay anywhere near as much as that. It's outrageous!'

'That's what I get for being a naughty girl and defying the big bad monster.' Emma gave a shaky laugh. 'Well, I was only saying to Tom last night that I'd probably have to look for new premises. Now it's a fact.'

'Oh, Emma, it's so unfair.'

'It's not unfair, Jenni. This is war. It's called retaliation.'

She went back into the shop and rang her solicitor, but, as she'd suspected, he was unable to do anything to help. Then she rang Tom and warned him they were in for trouble. For once he was unable to come up with any practical suggestions. He even went so far as to say he could understand del Sarto's reaction—after all, she had stuck her neck out—and she thanked him for that Libran remark and he apologised at once. 'I still think he's a scoundrel,' he told her. 'Let me make a few phone calls. There must be something we can do.'

After that she tried to get on with the rest of the day as if everything were normal. It was only when she had to make plans for the future, like agreeing to go out and look at a Victorian gateleg table someone had for sale, or arranging to hold on to some furniture for a customer until their builders had completed, that the difficulty of carrying on as normal hit her.

But she would not be beaten. When she got time she rang the grocer and the hairdresser. There she had another shock.

'He's allowing us to stay on even though my lease

expires next month. And I've had an offer of a place near
the town centre after that,' said the hairdresser, a young
man called Julian. 'My main worry was being thrown
out without anywhere to go. To be frank, Emma, this
new place will suit me better than here. My customers
very generously overlook the tattiness of the place I'm in
at present.'

The grocer was equally unhelpful. 'I've actually got a
half-promise of somewhere better, Emma. Still under
wraps, so I can't talk about it. But I'm sorry I'm not
going to be much use on the defence committee any
longer. I honestly don't think it would be worth my
while.'

Only after Emma put the phone down did she begin
to ponder the implication behind his words. 'Jack, is it
true,' she asked when she got through again, 'that del
Sarto is behind this offer of new premises you've had?'

The mumbled explanation at the other end confirmed
her suspicions.

Tom gave her a cuddle later on, stroking her dark hair
over and over again in a way that was intended to soothe.
'You can't blame him, Emma,' he said after she poured
out the latest move in the battle and called the grocer all
the names under the sun for what she saw as his betrayal.
'It does seem like a stab in the back, but Jack does have
his wife and children to think of. I must say, though, del
Sarto's a devious devil, buying him off like that.'

'Both of them. Julian too if my intuition is in working
order. Also Jenni in a way. He's given her another six
months with no increase in the lease, which means he's
not even taking inflation into account, so she's actually
paying less in real terms.' This seemed like Mark's final
treachery. When she pointed this out, Tom made some

less than helpful remark about her Cancerian concern for
money.

'The worst thing is,' he went on, 'he's isolated you,
hasn't he? And very cleverly too. There's not much you
can do against megabucks by yourself, chicken. I guess
you'll have to concede.'

'But what about the shop?' she argued. 'How can I
concede? Are you trying to tell me I have to let that rat
put me out of business?'

'There must be other premises. You simply haven't
made a concentrated search.'

'How can I?' she wailed. 'I have to run the shop! I
can't take time off to go trailing round looking at likely
alternatives. Especially not now, when I'm going to have
to find the extra to pay the higher premium.'

'I can't get around to help you on that score,' frowned
Tom, 'but I'll ring round all the estate agents first thing
in the morning and get them to send everything on their
books that might do.'

Emma imagined how much the phone bill would be
but forced herself not to say anything. All she allowed
was a plea that he leave his calls until the afternoon in
order to take advantage of the lower call-charge.

'You mustn't start worrying,' he squeezed her hand.
But she could see he was worried too. After all, there
were the payments on the house to keep up. Mark del
Sarto was exerting pressure in the most damaging way
he could.

Later Emma did some sums and worked out how much
the current shortfall would be, should her takings con-
tinue as they were at this rather quiet time of year and
should Mark insist that she pay up exactly on the due
date. It was humiliating to think that she might have to
go begging to the bank, but she kept that as a last resort.

The trouble was, she had overreached herself on her outgoings, spending a lot on some really fine purchases of furniture which she had got at bargain prices and knew she would be able to make a good profit on when she sold at the right time later in the year. By then, of course, with this unexpected demand, it would be too late. She would be out of business and, forced to sell too soon, even the profit she had been looking forward to would be cut to whatever she could get at the time. She was going to lose all round. And all due to Mark del Sarto.

Scraps of paper covered in figures were scattered all over the floor. None of it helped. No matter how carefully she went over them, it wouldn't work out.

Everything came back to Mark.

She could plead with him, of course. But she felt she would rather go out of business than humiliate herself like that. His smile of triumph would be a thorn in her side for the rest of her days. No, it was no good. She would not beg. She would simply have to find another way. A look at the figures again suggested a slim chance. Her trading figures had been generally good. If they picked up a little bit more, maybe it would all work out and she would manage to get over the hump.

That, she told herself gloomily, as she got ready to go in the next day after one of the longest nights of her life, was only to stave off the inevitable. Tom would never find an alternative. She knew the town well, and there was nothing, simply nothing, that could match the place she was already in.

Two days passed. As she'd expected, Tom had been unable to track down any premises that were even remotely suitable. Instead she took to adding up the figures and measuring the amount she still had to make before being forced to go to the bank. In fact, it wasn't looking too bad. With reasonable luck she would maybe just manage to hold him off.

Then came his next step in the campaign.

It was mid-morning and the postman had come in with his usual bundle of business mail. After standing chatting for a minute or two she glanced through the pile in her hand and suddenly felt her spirits plunge. There was another envelope with the del Sarto logo ominously embossed in one corner, and as soon as she saw it she scarcely gave the postman a goodbye before rushing through into the office to tear it open.

'In accordance with the terms of the lease the following repairs are now necessary,' she read. These, also according to the terms of the lease, were the responsibility of the lessee. This she already knew. She read on. There came a long list. Retiling of the roof, new guttering front and back, a couple of new windows, work to the chimney stack. . . the list was endless. It was utterly outrageous. Even a rough calculation told her that the sum for all this scrupulous refurbishment would run into thousands.

She crumpled the letter into a ball and gave way to tears. He was impossible. He knew she couldn't foot the bill. And under the terms of the lease that would mean she would be out. Overnight.

She gazed helplessly round at the stock. He couldn't force her out like this. But she knew he could. And would.

At once her mind began to churn over the practicalities. All the stock would have to go into storage—she would have to pay over the odds because, most of it valuable, it couldn't just be stacked up in a general warehouse with a lot of other things; and then there would be extra insurance premiums—the list was endless. She was going to lose from day one, any profit from subsequent sales being gradually eaten away. If she didn't find another shop, she was finished.

'I hate you from the bottom of my heart, Mark del Sarto,' she whispered in the privacy of her office. She felt like tearing the place apart with her bare hands. That would show him what she thought of him. She gritted her teeth. He would also no doubt land her with an almighty bill for damage caused, too!

He had caught her well and truly in his trap. Now her pathetic figures designed to keep her head above water and the prospect of the mild humiliation of having to go to the bank for an overdraft seemed nothing compared to this.

She went to a drawer of her desk and took out her copy of the lease. After reading it through twice she knew it was useless. She was legally liable for any bills until the lease ran out. So, even if she refused to have the work done, Mark was entitled to come in, have it fixed, and then charge her with all the expense.

Why, oh, why did I sign such an unfair document? she fumed. But in the old days, the leisurely, un-businesslike days before Mark took over, everything had been done on the basis of friendly agreement. A situation like this would never have arisen.

The shop was depressingly empty at half-past three when Mark himself at last put in an appearance.

She had known he would come sooner or later, and now he strode over the threshold like a conquering warlord. Emma rose to meet him, stopping halfway down the aisle near an ormolu cabinet, head erect, her pride giving her the semblance of control she needed to face him.

She didn't offer any greeting, and when he came to a stop in front of her she gave him one look that spoke volumes. It made no impression on him, of course, though he concealed his triumph under his usual impassive exterior.

'I take it you got my letter.'

'You mean that list of ridiculous repairs?'

He didn't contradict, but merely nodded his black head.

'Thank you, Mr del Sarto. You play dirty, don't you? I wonder if you manage to sleep at night?' She turned and rested one hand on the marble-topped cabinet in a search for stability. Her hands were shaking but she forced herself to still them. It was a beautiful piece of furniture. Now she would never know the real pleasure of seeing it go to someone who appreciated it as much as she did. It would finish up in a sale-room, sold impersonally to a stranger. She fought back the tears.

'You wanted a fight and you've got it,' he grated in her ear.

'Yes.' She raised her head and gave him a bleak glance. 'Any other surprises for me? Perhaps you've got plans to bulldoze the house I live in, too? After all, it's near enough to be included in your game of Monopoly, isn't it?'

'Don't be silly. I'm not in the business of putting people on to the streets.'

'No?' She gave a thin smile. Her heart was beginning to racket uncontrollably. If he didn't leave at once she would probably do something she regretted. She felt her face change colour with the exertion of fighting down the conflicting emotions he aroused.

'I can help you,' he said tonelessly. 'If you ask me, I'll help you.'

'You will? May I enquire into the methods and purpose of such help?'

He looked relaxed and in control when he said, 'There

are one or two possibilities that spring to mind.' He gave
a faint smile. 'One of the more acceptable to you would
be to reconsider the commission to refurbish my house
for me. We haven't talked figures but I can guarantee
the going rate is more than generous. It would offset the
necessary expense this property requires.'

'Tell me one thing, Mr del Sarto: why should I trust
you?'

'You have no option,' he replied at once. 'Do you still
imagine you have a choice in this? I've got you cornered
and you'll have to accept that. Or lose everything.'

'These repairs——' She gestured wildly around the
shop. 'Why should you insist on having it repaired when
it's going to be pulled down?'

'That's by no means an open and shut issue. Granted
it won't be kept in its present state. This place is pretty
enough, but the block itself is a public eyesore, as I'm
sure most of the good citizens in this town will agree,
despite your efforts to persuade them otherwise in the
pages of the local Press. But I aim to rectify that.
Whether by pulling it down or simply restoring it to its
former grandeur as a coaching inn, I have yet to decide.'

'I see.'

'Do you?' He moved a step forward, his voice roughening. 'If you see, then you'll realise you have to accept
my help.'

'Work for you?' Her scathing voice would have made
a less confident mortal falter.

But Mark merely shrugged. 'I think once you've gone
over the figures you'll see it makes sense. I know figures
are important to you, so I had this made out.'

He handed her a document wallet embossed with the
del Sarto logo, and on opening it she discovered several
pages of detailed accounts showing what could be spent
on the house, in what way, and what percentage she

herself would get for seeing the job through. When she came to the final figure she couldn't restrain a bitter smile. It matched the sum likely to be needed to repair the shop premises.

'Neat. I'll give you that. Congratulate your accountant for me. But why, Mark, why?'

His face was tight with some emotion. 'Has he moved out?' he demanded.

'He?' She couldn't understand what he was getting at, then it slowly dawned on her. He was asking her about Tom, still under the misapprehension that he was her live-in lover or something of the sort.

'Well?' he demanded savagely, his feelings cracking to the surface in a sudden eruption. He moved a step nearer but she stepped away, crossing to the opposite side of the aisle until her retreat was hindered by the corner of a roll-top desk.

'Why should I have to tell you anything like that? What's it got to do with you?' Her voice was hoarse.

With an effort he seemed to bring his emotions under control. She could see him visibly fight them back. The moment was over in a trice, but Emma felt shaken at the idea that he was still thinking along those lines. What did it mean? He seemed to hate her. She was simply a thorn in his side, obstructing his grandiose schemes, refusing to play his game. So why this odd, desperate, defeated look, an almost murderous rage, barely under control?

In any other man it might have spelled jealousy. But it couldn't mean that with him. They hadn't got that sort of relationship. An image of how things had been when they had been at the country house that day came back to remind her how, despite their edginess, there had been something scarcely controlled below the surface then as well. She hadn't understood it then either, but now she recalled what he had told her—he was a man prone to dark obsessions for what he didn't possess. She had thought it was simply a form of words. Now she was in confusion.

She heard him say, 'I'm going to be out of town for a day or two. You've got until Friday.' Without another word he was gone.

Later, when she came to reread the proposal for the work he wanted doing at the house, she was impressed by his thoroughness—or, she corrected, that of his staff—and she showed the papers to Tom.

After reading them through he turned to her with a beam. 'That's great. So he's not so bad after all.'

Emma wondered what it was that had made her suddenly feel old. Then she knew. Tom was in love with Angelika. He was looking at everything through rose-coloured lenses. While she, not under any sort of starry illusion like love, could see the world in all its monstrous ugliness.

Part of that ugliness was Mark del Sarto's revenge. He wanted her—for some punishing reason to do with sex or possession, she didn't know which, only that it definitely wasn't love—and his way of making sure he got her was first to push her to the edge of financial ruin, then to offer an apparently helping hand.

Once she accepted his help—as, indeed, she was being forced to do—she would be completely within his power.

It was a reprieve he offered her, certainly, but one which held within it the seed of her ultimate defeat.

CHAPTER EIGHT

IT WAS two days of hell. From the moment Mark left the shop after his ultimatum Emma knew the next step was inevitable. What choice had she? Her mind twisted and turned like a butterfly in a net in an effort to escape. But it was no good. There was no way out.

When the two days were up she set off for the shop in a state of deepest misery. Everything was finished. She could only walk blindly down the street, aware that every step took her closer to losing everything she had. All right, so there was going to be a three-month reprieve, but after that she would be back with her whole future on the line again, just as it had been.

It was a hand on her shoulder that brought her back to the present.

'I called after you three times.' It was Mark. He seemed taller, leaner, and somehow more formidable than before. Looking up at him, Emma saw how unyielding he was, and whatever brief fantasy she had had of appealing to his better nature would, she saw clearly, have no chance of penetrating such rock-hard resistance.

'Lost in thought.' It was neither a question nor a statement but a kind of file-heading under which he would now docket his impressions of her ensuing actions. Requiring no answer, he walked on in silence towards the shop.

No doubt he expects me to follow two paces behind, she thought bitterly, noting the long stride, the power, the physical excess of the man. She felt utterly defeated, cringing inside herself, made small by him, and trailing along at far more than the regulation two paces, aware of both an irrational desire to follow him and a quite rational hatred towards him for expecting her to do so.

By the time she reached the shop he was waiting for her in the doorway, and his expression plainly told her that he thought she had been trying to score some small victory by keeping him waiting. She was too listless to counter this impression. It made no difference now. He was here to collect. It was a game of Monopoly where one player won everything and the other contestants retreated in total disarray. It was almost funny, she thought, as she unlocked the door. As a child she had always won at board games. Maybe that was why this defeat hurt so much. She had never learned how to be a good loser.

He must have noticed her slight smile.

'So you've got something up your sleeve, have you?' He followed her in and closed the door behind them and they stood in the darkness among the perfumed wood and the pale glimmer of reflected light.

'Me? No, how could I have? You've closed all exits for me.'

'I wondered if you'd manage to think your way out of it? I wouldn't put it past you.'

'How could I have?' she asked defeatedly. 'What could I have done? You've made it impossible for me to turn down your commission. I can't afford to have all those repairs done to this place without that and you know it. If I don't do them, I'm still liable should you insist.'

'And I will.'

'Oh, I'm in no doubt about that!' She knew there was more at stake than merely working on the house for him. But he was keeping up the pretence that it was purely a business matter between them. 'What else can I do but accept your offer?' she repeated, as if to set the matter straight in her own mind.

'You can't do anything else, if you want to keep your business as a going concern.' He gave a smug smile. 'But life is full of surprises. You might have found some way of wriggling out of it.'

'I'm not full of surprises. I'm very predictable.'

'You'll guarantee that, will you? I like to know where I am.'

'What sort of guarantee do you want?' She smiled without energy. 'It's your game, Mr del Sarto. You call the shots from now on.'

'Yes, I do, don't I?' He looked pleased.

'So what now?' She shrugged. It was all the same to her.

'Why do you look so depressed about it? I've offered you help. Now you see you can't proceed without it, you should be delighted—you've got a way out. You can keep your shop until the future of the whole block is settled and it won't cost you a thing.'

When she didn't react, even to this, he repeated, 'You can keep it now.'

'Yes, I can, can't I? And it won't cost?' She jerked away but his hand came out, forcing her round again.

His lips were pale but the colour of his face was even paler. 'Are you saying the price is too high?'

'For me, yes. Any price I have to render you would be too high. And especially the one you're asking now.'

She felt his fingers tighten but his expression didn't alter.

'What a pity,' he said evenly. 'It's the first rule of business that everyone pays at some time.'

'Do you?' She raised her head.

'Yes, Emma, I'm paying now.' Before she could ask him what he meant, he let his hand drop and turned roughly, making his way down between the rows of furniture to her office. She watched as, without a word of permission, he went straight inside and took a seat on the far side of her desk.

When she followed his manner had changed. He was curt and businesslike, and she knew it was the wrong time to demand an explanation for his strange words just now.

He said, 'My men are coming in here to start work next week. Obviously it will be pointless to try to cope with customers at the same time as builders are tramping in and out, so you'll have to close and some of the better pieces will be put in storage——'

'But I——'

'I know you don't want to afford it, as a Cancer sign, but I'm sure you can pay easily enough for the few pieces I've listed here.' He delved into his briefcase and took out a file. 'There's a second page,' he pointed out as she scanned the top sheet. 'Those things listed on page one will come on loan to one of my houses. I'll pay insurance, of course, and you may be certain there'll be no chance of them coming to any harm——'

'But——' she began again.

'The rest, the less valuable things listed on the second page, will be packed by my people before they start work. Now, while this place is more or less out of action you'll work on restoring the inside of Larwood Hall to its former glory. Any questions?'

'But——' she began again, then let her protests trail away. It was all so cut and dried that she felt like a cog in a machine, no will of her own required. All she had to do was fall in with what he wanted. She frowned. 'Seems you've worked out all the angles.' She glanced down at the two lists he had given her. 'You've even chosen the best pieces. How did you do that?'

'I'm not a fool.'

'Is that an explanation or an excuse?' She couldn't resist a smile but she avoided his glance. It was all unreal. 'And when I've finished working on the house—Larwood, is it?'

He nodded.

'What then?'

'Who knows? Anything might have happened by then.'

She raised her brows.

'I guess it should take about three months. Assuming all the contractors are reliable and——'

'Three months?' She broke in with a gasp. That was when the future of the whole building came up again. Would she lose her shop and come to the end of the Larwood job both at the same time? Then what?

'It's long enough, isn't it?'

'It depends,' she remarked drily. She would not let him see how frightened she felt. She gave a shrug and a half-smile.

'That's better.'

'What is?'

'You. Almost your old self. I was worried about you when I met you just now in the street.'

'You don't know my old self.'

'No. But the past is always with us, isn't it?'

'Is it?'

'So it would seem.' He gave her a level glance. There was a pause. Then he stretched out his long legs and got up from his place behind the desk and came over to her. 'I hope you appreciate what I'm doing for you, Emma.'

'Why should I? You're only doing it for the ultimate good of Mark del Sarto. I'm purely incidental.'

'Are you?'

'Nothing could be more obvious.'

For a moment his glance seemed to penetrate her own with something on the brink of revelation, but he made a small movement of his head as if he was drawing back from that forbidden threshold again. 'Anyway,' he said, in an offhand sort of way that didn't prepare her for his next shock, 'you'll have to live on site and, as I want to get things moving as quickly as possible, I can give you till tomorrow morning to sort things out.'

'On site?' She stared at him, not understanding.

'At Larwood, of course. There's a perfectly adequate annexe, if you remember, and it should be in reasonably good order by now.'

'But I can't live there!' Her eyes opened wide.

'Give me one good reason?'

'Why——' In her confusion she could only think of one other one after the big one of wanting to have as little to do with the del Sarto empire as possible, and it could be expressed in one word. 'Tom,' she said.

There was silence. Mark's face looked greyish in the north light streaming through the window. He didn't move.

'Well, I mean. . . I can't and that's that. . .' She stared back at him. Why wasn't he arguing with her? He was simply staring. It was frightening. He looked so cold.

His voice when it came seemed to emanate from a distance, grinding out the words in a pitchless way that made her think he was already assessing other schemes with which to entrap her should this one prove insuperable. 'I thought,' he said, 'that was all over. I thought you'd seen sense and thrown him out. Or that he'd gone off with your best friend or your best piece of jewellery. That day you were in tears, you gave me the impression it was over.'

'I gave you no impression, at least, not deliberately. Why should I? What's it to do with you who I live with?'

'Anyway——' he got up and went to the door, his voice recovering its normal tone '——he'll have to find somebody else to perform whatever services you customarily perform for him——'

'Wait!' Red rage flooded her vision. This was too much. All she wanted was to stop him. Drag him back. Make him turn, understand how things really were between her and Tom.

Somehow she was plucking at the sleeve of his jacket, then her fingers found his arm and closed round it and her other hand came up, to do what she hadn't considered, but he jerked round as if blocking an attack, gripping her wrist and ramming her arm down while at the same time fending off her other hand which was following the first. This time he was less lucky and her fist caught him on the side of the head. She recoiled at the touch of his skin beneath her clenched fingers. Then recoiled even further as he lunged forward, forcing her against the wall, the full weight of his lethally strong body crushing the breath from her.

Then it was like a blaze of fireworks, a sudden conflagration of desire as he enveloped her in his arms and forced his lips down over hers. Heat raced between them like firecrackers, his tongue forcing its way into her mouth, her own responding with an urgency she had never felt before as the desire to take his heat into her swept over her.

She felt her body melt, trembling against him, her softness, her yielding matched by his hardness and purpose.

Then his kisses became stronger, more desperate, demanding, rising to the brink of anger. She gasped at the fierceness of his touch, at the way his teeth bit into the softness of her lips, but before she could succumb to this difference he lifted his head, gave a groan of something like dismay at his own weakness and with every sign of knowing exactly what he was doing moved back, severing the contact between them.

'What the hell——?' He pretended to smile but she saw clearly that it didn't reach his eyes. One hand came up to the side of his face where she had hit him and he gave another more rueful grimace as he fingered it. 'You pack a powerful punch, Miss Shields. Now would you tell me what it was for?'

'You know damn well,' she muttered still unable to collect her racing thoughts.

'I touched a raw nerve, did I? How was I to know you were so touchy about him?' He was pretending it was all over, that his kiss had been an accident of some sort, or that it hadn't happened. He touched his cheekbone again. 'If this is you being predictable we'd better have a written guarantee there'll be no all-out fights for three months. I'm not sure it's on to have bruises all over my face at my age. It wouldn't be good for business.'

'On the contrary,' she spat, cloaking her real feelings beneath a mantle of ice, 'it would let people know exactly what they were in for, dealing with you!'

He actually smiled. 'I knew we were well matched.' He reached out and touched her on the shoulder. 'Come on. You're not going to do anything here today. I'll walk you back and you can go and tell that man of yours how to boil an egg. You've got till tomorrow to show him what he needs to know to look after himself——'

'Not so fast!' She backed out of his reach. 'You're making a hell of a lot of assumptions here. First, I haven't said I'll move into this Larwood place. Second, you know nothing about Tom. Not one solitary damned thing, and you've no right to talk about him in that horrible disparaging way, and third——'

'Hold it.' He bulked over her but without actually raising a hand to touch her. 'You have no choice about coming to Larwood. I need you there. And that's final. And as for the rest, a man who relies on a woman to keep him is no sort of man in my view. Doesn't he mind that you're worried out of your head over your little business? If he cared a damn about you he'd at least take some of the financial responsibility off you. Share it. That's what partnerships are about. Sharing. Nobody deserves a free ride.'

Emma opened her mouth then closed it. Now would be the time to put him right about Tom. But why should she? She had seen what he was like just now, and he would no doubt only go on making caustic remarks about malingerers, or make some mocking reference to their love-life or rather lack of it. He was hateful enough to say anything. It would break her heart to hear such things said about darling Tom. Tears came into her eyes.

'Waterworks,' he observed cynically. 'You're a water sign so I guess it's reasonable. You certainly run true to form.'

Now the tears were streaming down both cheeks and she couldn't stop them.

'Hey.' He reached out and rubbed the side of her face with the backs of his fingers. 'Come on, it's not as bad as that. Is it what I've just said about lover-boy? You know it's true, don't you. That's the problem. I guess it's hard to take the truth about somebody you've been sharing a sort of marriage with. Come on, Emma. This isn't like you. You're one tough little lady. You've certainly given me a run for my money. . .'

He looped his arms around her shoulders before she could summon up the energy to resist, then he was pressing his lips against the side of her hair in a gentle, reassuring way quite unlike the fierce taking with which he had only just now kissed her into confusion.

'Better?' he murmured against her ear, dropping light kisses on to it. 'Some things have to be faced. . . OK?' He looked down at her, eyes laser-bright, so bright as to conceal what emotion if any was driving him to treat her gently now he'd got her where he wanted her.

She gave a stifled sob, 'It's not really like that.' Standing in his arms, his male presence overpowering her, she found that all thought of explaining things to him was sent spinning away out of reach. He could hold her like this forever, she was thinking, swaying a little in his arms—except for that strand of common sense that made sure she would never quite forget he was a cold, conniving, ruthless type after all. And all he was doing now was trying to soften her up so that she would fall meekly in with his plans.

'I'll walk you back. Maybe I shall have a word with him.' He smiled as if the idea was a new one, and when he went on smiling she wondered what was brewing next.

She allowed him to turn her and shepherd her towards the door. He had picked up her keys and took over the locking of the door before walking beside her down the street in the direction of the house—and in the direction of the unsuspecting Tom.

When they came to the row of Victorian houses where Mark had previously left her, Emma slowed. She had to make a decision and stick to it. 'I can handle this myself, Mark. There's no need for you to come in.'

'You mean you want me to lurk around outside the house like a felon?'

'Don't you have business to attend to?' she asked.

'Let me speak to him. I'll sort him out.' He wore a truculent expression.

But she still insisted. 'I do have some say in this deal, don't I? Surely the days when the servants had no choice in anything are over now?'

He tightened his jaw. 'Don't you trust me? Do you think I'll be too blunt? Maybe,' he grimaced, 'you imagine I intend to follow your example and punch him in the face?'

'For heaven's sake! Why should you do a thing like that? You've cornered me into working for you for three months. Why should that lead to anybody punching anybody else?'

'You're right. It would look like a crime of passion.'

'I hope it's not going to be a crime of any sort!' she exclaimed.

Despite her apparent control, all her misgivings were rising to the surface. How on earth was she going to handle her emotions for three whole months if they couldn't even stand talking in the shop for more than five minutes without finding themselves in each other's arms? They would run out of excuses to keep apart. And then what? She wouldn't become his mistress. She would not. But if he insisted? How long could she hold out? His kiss just now had been the most powerful experience of her life. Already she was longing to be in his arms again.

But it was madness to allow such thoughts. He was a cold, conniving snake, without an ounce of feeling for her—except for this sexual obsession now only too plain to see. She sneaked a look at him but he was glowering up at the house as if willing it to burst into flames together with its innocent occupant.

She shuddered at the realisation that she knew little about him other than that he was fabulously wealthy and seemed to have all the local businessmen in his pocket. There was only one thing she did know for certain—his brooding, obsessional side spelled danger.

But now he was pacing at the bottom of the steps.

'I'm going in,' she told him abruptly. 'You promised you'd give me a day to sort things out. Tomorrow you can pick me up at nine. Unless,' she couldn't resist adding, 'you intend to start work any earlier?'

He gave a faint smile. 'I expect nine will do.'

'Good. Then that's that.'

She turned before he could delay her with any more objections which she couldn't counter, and ran up the steps, her hand already groping in her bag for the key so that she was able to let herself inside with scarcely a pause. As she closed the door he was standing where she had left him at the bottom of the steps, gazing after her with the same brooding expression, giving his handsome face an even greater air of threat.

'Tom,' she called as soon as she got inside, shutting out the picture, 'you must save me! The most horrible thing has happened and——' By now she was on the threshold of the sitting-room and here she jerked to a stop. Tom was lying on the day-bed with his shirt off and a tall, red-haired woman leaning over him, massaging his back with strong, measured strokes. She raised her head and smiled when Emma went on staring in at them both, then continued with what she was doing.

'I'm sorry——' Emma said automatically, then pulled herself up. What was she doing, apologising for walking into her own house? But there was such a cosy air about the two of them that for a second she felt like an intruder. Now Tom was lifting his head too.

'Caught in the act!' He twisted so he was half reclining against some cushions and took hold of the stranger's

hand. 'Meet my physio, Angelika. No,' he corrected
with a grin. 'Meet Angelika, my love.'

Emma went across. 'I see you've managed to get him
under control at last. Something I never quite managed.'

She shook hands, then began to turn towards the door.

'Hey,' Tom called her back. 'What was all that noise
drifting my way just now?'

'Noise?'

'You were shouting about something as you came in.'

'Oh, it was nothing.' She bit her lip.

'I've finished with you for now, Tommy. I think I'll
go and make some tea.' Angelika pulled Tom's bathrobe
from under the cushions and wrapped it professionally
round his shoulders.

'Oh, I didn't mean it was anything private——' began
Emma in confusion.

'She's labouring under the sign of Cancer,' explained
Tom to Angelika as if Emma wasn't there. 'Secretive,
worrying types. Like to keep their troubles to themselves. But absolute darlings once they feel secure.'

Angelika and Emma exchanged glances. 'I'll still get
that drink.' She made for the door.

When she'd gone Emma sank down on the edge of the
day bed. 'She seems to know where the kitchen is,' she
observed. 'And she's nice. I like her.'

'Good. That means a lot to me. It's reassuring to have
a second opinion. My judgement probably isn't as balanced as it used to be.'

'Nothing wrong with your judgement,' she quipped.

As she got up to go he pulled her back. 'So what is it?
What was all that about just now?'

'Oh, Tom.' She sank down again, legs suddenly weak.
'I don't know which way to turn. Every route is blocked
by that—what is he? That monster,' she answered her
own question. 'He just assumes he can barge in and run

people's lives for them. And I don't know how to fight him. I can't fight—but I know I have to. And now this latest scheme—it's impossible—I feel——' She broke off. She couldn't tell Tom how frightened she felt, nor why.

But he took her by the hand. 'Now why don't you start at the beginning and explain everything in an orderly way. Starting,' he warned when he saw her face pucker, 'with when you went out this morning less than an hour ago.'

'He came up as I was walking to the shop——' she began. And then she told him everything, or almost everything, and as she was talking Angelika came in with a tray and put a mug of scalding hospital tea into her hand and when she finally came to the end both she and Tom exclaimed at once how appalling Mark del Sarto was to behave in such a high-handed fashion.

Tom then went on to qualify a statement like that. 'It sounds a good scheme in financial terms for the pair of you. I mean, even you have to admit that this is the worst time of year for the shop. In January to March, you're always saying, you may as well be closed.'

'Maybe that's not what's worrying her,' suggested Angelika with a glance at Emma. The two women exchanged looks.

'So it's me, is it?' Tom frowned. 'What did he say when you explained you had a cripple to look after?'

'Tom, I won't hear you say that sort of thing——' Emma forced back the tears. Then she had to admit that she hadn't got around to a full explanation. 'I don't see why I should tell him all about us——'

Tom raised his eyebrows.

'He's a brute, Tom. I can't have him make scathing comments—oh, please, don't make me explain any more.'

'It's all right.' Tom patted her hand. 'They're loyal too, these Cancerians,' he explained to Angelika in an aside. 'Even when there's no need for it.'

Emma didn't know how to go on. Yes, what she had just hinted was true, she couldn't be disloyal to Tom, but there was also the other issue—the fact that she didn't want to go to Larwood Hall and spend all that time in close proximity with Mark del Sarto. Because she didn't trust him. And, worse, didn't trust herself.

Finally she was forced to admit it—his dark side held a fascination for her. It was the fascination of a flame for a child, of something dangerous which one could not leave alone. But now Tom was telling her she must find a solution and accept the job, enter the danger zone, though he didn't see it like that, couldn't in fact see it like that, and didn't understand what it was he was encouraging her to face.

She got up. 'It's obviously not practical anyway,' she said conclusively. 'I'm not leaving you for anything. So that's that.'

But then Angelika leaned forward. 'I know this is probably dreadfully forward of me, but what about this for a suggestion?' She looked nervously from Tom to Emma, then said hurriedly, 'I mean if you think the idea's preposterous you only have to say.'

'Nothing you say is ever preposterous,' remarked Tom fondly. 'Go on.'

'Well, it's this. If Emma needs to be at this Larwood Hall during the week, why couldn't I live here? Paying rent, of course, to help out with the mortgage. My work with the agency is entirely up to me—I choose when and where I work. . .well,' she said, watching their faces, 'it was just an idea.'

★ ★ ★

Next morning, while Angelika waved goodbye from the front steps, Emma followed Mark out to the car. She should have felt pleased that at least on one count things had turned out well, for she knew Tom was now in good hands. But instead, of course, she was terrified.

When they were in the car Mark glowered across at her and the carefully imagined shreds of optimism she had been nurturing since breakfast vanished like the chimeras they were. Brute reality forced its way in. Ahead lay problems. Number one loomed straight in front.

'So?' he demanded. 'How did he take it?'

'Does it matter?'

His nerves seemed wound up like steel wires ready to snap. 'You should have made a clean break before instead of letting it drag on like this.' A nerve jumped in his jaw. 'I shouldn't have had to force you to it.'

'Is that how you see it?' She felt equally wound up and her voice sounded hard, without its usual soft timbre. 'You see yourself forcing me to reorganise my love-life?' She gave a hard laugh. 'You don't know what you're talking about!'

He slammed the car into gear and forced a van behind to brake sharply as he pulled into the stream of traffic. He drove in total silence all the way out of town, passing the waterfront with his name blazoned on all the boards round the new construction site, and joining the ring road with a sudden swoop of speed that seemed to underline the fact that she was being driven far out of reach of help and the sanity of ordinary life.

She felt her limbs turn to ice at the prospect of what lay ahead, and by the time they reached Larwood Hall she felt mentally and emotionally numb.

As the car pulled up, she had convinced herself that whatever happened she would give nothing away about her personal life. Mark would tear it to shreds and try to make nothing of the years she and Tom had shared. But it represented the good and the real. Something she could hang on to in the weeks that lay ahead. Something pure and inviolable. Something Mark del Sarto would never reach.

She remembered Tom's astrology and what he had told her recently about the difficulties she would have in finding agreement with colleagues, and ruefully admitted to herself that he had been right. He had also told her she would enter a good phase for romance. On that score he had been laughably wrong!

'I wonder what sign you are, after all?' She eyed him coldly as she climbed out of the car.

'Me?' He seemed to relax for a moment. 'Scorpio, of course, didn't you guess?'

She turned her head when she reached the inner door leading into the entrance hall and looked at him over her shoulder. 'That figures,' she said without further explanation.

Scorpio. The soft approach, then the whiplash. She wondered if she could hold out. Would her strength match his?

He held the door, and as she brushed past him she saw his brooding expression as his glance rested on her face. Then he followed after her like a black spectre pursuing her into the depths of the house.

CHAPTER NINE

THERE were staff in the house already. A secretary and a couple of assistants and various other people in overalls. After they had been introduced in an ante-room set aside as an office while the work was in progress, Mark led Emma to the annexe. He even carried her bag for her. He dumped it down in the doorway of the rooms she had been alloted, then took her by the arm. 'So what was that supposed to mean?'

'What?' She wanted to struggle but found the unexpectedness of the physical contact, which she should have been prepared for, eating at once into her will.

She felt her knees begin to tremble. It was ridiculous, she tried to tell herself. He was only holding her by the arm. Only gazing into her eyes with that intent stare as if he could see into her soul. . . only bringing his lips close. . . only. . . but she had to resist.

'What does what mean?'

'That comment about my sun sign,' he said throatily without coming any closer.

'Nothing, Mark. I wasn't thinking——' She slipped out of his grip and bent to fiddle with the clasp of her bag on the floor.

'Liar.' He came closer. 'You never stop thinking. One day maybe you'll start feeling as well.'

'I feel a lot,' she whispered, as he came right up to her and put his arms on her shoulders as she straightened. She was scarcely able to think at all when he came as close as this. It was like an embrace, but not quite that. One tiny movement could separate them. They hovered

143

on the edge, danger and the siren song beckoning them to go a little further.

His lips twisted. 'I wonder how you're going to feel about him after three months' separation?'

He was back to that again. She said, 'It won't be three months' separation. I shall go back at weekends.'

'We'll see.'

'What on earth do you mean?' Her voice came out as a whisper again.

'We'll be working round the clock.'

'It's against the law——'

'Don't quote regulations at me; you're self-employed, freelance, you work how and whenever necessary. I know. I've been through it.' His hands were still on her shoulders.

'Have you?' She didn't know what she was saying but could feel her glance seek hungrily over his face as if by doing so she could learn something about him, something that would help her defend herself against him, something that would help her draw back from the dangerous brink on which they stood. But his expression was as always impenetrable.

'I wasn't born into this, Emma. I've had to work my way to this point. My father had an ice-cream business—don't laugh. We're second-generation Italians from Amalfi. My brothers went into the family business. They're all married with a brace of sons apiece. I was the one who branched out.' He gave a satisfied smile. 'I'm ambitious. Mean. Is that what you're thinking? Well, you're right. I am both of those. Nobody stands in my way, as you've recently discovered. Now, what else did you want to say that figures?'

Weakly she shook her head. 'You've said it, and what you haven't said we both know.'

'That I'm a bastard? Yes. Why not? I've had to fight.

It comes naturally. I enjoy it. I like winning. I want the best. And I damn well make sure I get it.'

'Good for you.' Her eyes matched his in arrogance for a moment and she saw something kindle within his grey ones before his head came down as it was predestined to do.

When he'd finished with her lips he murmured in a hoarse voice, 'You're the best in a long while, Emma, and I'm going to have you too. That's how ambitious I am. I know you don't care a damn. Why should you? I nearly broke you. But you shouldn't have tried to fight me. You were warned. And that goes for this as well—if you fight, I'll break you again. Only next time there'll be no reprieve.'

With a feeling of doom she felt him take her into his arms. There was nothing to stop him doing with her what he wanted. Nothing except her own will to resist.

If there was no reprieve, at least this time there was a respite, for there was much work to be done by both of them. The entire house was buzzing with activity, and although the annexe, sprawling with rooms Mark had already had refitted as offices and living quarters, was set to one side of the main building, there was a constant coming and going of staff between the two.

Mark spent the rest of the day in consultation with colleagues on his personal phone and Emma found herself in sole charge of operations in the house. Measurements had to be made, colour samples and swatches of fabrics jigsawed into suitable arrangements, costings made. All of it would take time. She saw the practical common sense of living on site as she began to organise her work schedule.

Towards the middle of the afternoon, Mark left the house in the silver bullet of a car, with only a couple of parallels in the deep gravel of the drive to show he'd ever been there. Someone told her he had gone to London. They said it in such a way that she guessed this was a normal occurrence, and wouldn't have been surprised if they had said he had gone to Paris or New York in exactly the same tone.

Later, when work was over for the day, he had still not returned, but she had supper, cooked and served by someone employed for the job, sharing with the others who were also living on site. She was relieved to find she was not to be lodged out here alone. Or, as she'd feared, alone with Mark.

They had finished eating and the others were making moves to walk down to the village pub to round things off when Emma suddenly realised how tired she was. Declining their invitation, she said she would take a stroll round the garden then turn in early.

After they left she let herself out into the twilit grounds. It was wrong to call it a garden because, she had discovered, the garden she had already seen was only a small part of the whole estate. There was land on all sides, woodland, a walled kitchen garden, a rose garden much in need of attention, and a lake.

'Take the path beside the caravans and walk on through the wood,' advised Mark's assistant before he left. 'It's a pretty walk to the lake.'

Some of the staff had had to be housed in three vans out of sight in the shrubberies. Only Mark's assistant, an accountant named John, was staying in one of the annexe rooms.

She followed his instructions and sure enough, after a short stroll along a path between two hedges of yew, came to an iron kissing-gate, then the clipped grass and flower-beds gave way to waist-high grass, sedge and bulrushes bordering a tranquil stretch of blue water. As she approached, a shower of wild geese rose up from the reeds and flew off with a clacking of wings.

It was beautiful. Emma sat down on a hump of stone near the water's edge and let her thoughts drift.

Scorpio. She gazed over to the other side of the lake without really seeing it. What would Tom say about Scorpio? He had told her they were well matched. She shuddered. It wasn't what she felt at all. His brooding violence frightened her. She felt that one false step would lead her crashing over into something terrible. She had felt like this from the first. But, whenever it had threatened before, she had been able to retreat. Or he had retreated, as if he knew it was useless to push on any further.

Now he had brought her here, did it mean he had changed his opinion? That he was willing to dip into the forbidden, risk the latent fires that might break into life and consume them both? She shuddered. Three months seemed a long time in which to play about on the brink of something so potentially destructive.

There was a sound behind her. Turning her head she felt the world come to a momentary standstill. He was there at the kissing gate, his clothes light, almost luminous in the twilight, his hair black as night, his expression saying anything she cared to read into it.

He began to wade through the long grass towards her. 'I guessed you might be out here.'

'I might have been with the others in the pub,' she told him.

'You?' He reached out to touch the top of her head where she sat. She felt a tremor run through her. He pulled her to her feet and took her unresistingly into his arms. It seemed like the most natural thing in the world when he said, 'Beautiful Emma,' and kissed her like a long-absent lover, with familiarity, hunger, care, and an air of utter certainty that very soon they would be lovers.

'Oh, Mark,' she whispered, trembling uncontrollably against him. The arms which held her seemed reassuring, pressing her against him with a gentleness to which she longed to surrender.

Without a word they sauntered slowly round the lake. They didn't indulge in small talk. There was no need for words somehow. It was as if everything could be said by touch, or by some other means as in a magical symbiosis, making verbal communication irrelevant. She was conscious of every little thing about him, the texture of his shirt beneath her fingers, the hardness of his muscled back, the warmth and smoothness of the fingers touching the inside of her wrist, the height and width of his shoulders on a level with her lips, the length of his stride as they paced the edge together.

When they reached the statue of Venus at the other end they paused and he turned her in the most natural way so that they were facing into each other. He seemed to refocus with an effort, then said, 'Think you can resign yourself to being here with me?'

She lowered her lashes in silent acquiescence.

Resign herself?

The whole sky seemed bright with love for them. But it wasn't love, was it? She knew that. Only the weakness that came from longing passionately for something made her yearn to change their battle of wills into something gentle.

But he was beginning to smooth his hands over her body in a way that was becoming increasingly masterful. At first just a light skimming movement, it became stronger as if he was being driven by something deep within. She felt her body become pliant, moulding itself to the contours of his arching body as he bent her back in his arms. Her head tilted, lips opening, and she gave a shuddering breath as a fiery tide swept from the soles of her feet into the roots of the hair on her head when his mouth enveloped hers in a kiss that turned itself into a mark of possession.

'Give me your tongue,' he husked. A flame swept through her again as she allowed this taking, his hot mouth drawing from her a stream of sensations, a tide of exquisite pleasure taking her, wordlessly telling her that this was how it was meant to be.

She was falling, flying, with no care for the danger of it, turning and falling in his arms, into love, into the abyss.

It was night.

While they embraced by the lake, the sun had hovered on the horizon, transforming the skeletons of the trees into black lacework and the pewter of the water to gold. Then every ounce of colour was drawn down below the rim of the earth into an enveloping darkness. There was a sense of frost in the air and the stars came out.

Mark wrapped his arms round her shoulders, turning her towards the lights of the house, holding her close against him as if to share his body heat. 'Emma, come back with me now.'

She knew he meant more than a mere invitation to go back indoors. In a dream she allowed him to lead her towards the inevitable. Nothing else was said. Nothing needed to be said. But when she looked at him neither his expression nor his caresses showed how he felt at the approaching fulfilment of desire.

Was he triumphant at the knowledge that she was about to submit? What did he feel? she wondered. Was he as nervous as she was at the prospect of giving in to the demon that had swept them into its grasp?

Did he feel as helpless as she did in the face of fortune?

As driven by the urgency of desire to possess her as she
was at the prospect of being possessed? She wanted to
delay their headlong rush towards the inevitable but he
hurried her along as if driven beyond restraint, striding
through the corridors of the night without a pause.

He led her straight to his room. It was large and
sparsely furnished, French windows giving on to a
secluded corner of the garden. She watched him draw
heavy curtains across the windows and go round adjust-
ing the lights until there was only one left to supplement
the flickering firelight and the strange shadows it cast
over the ceiling.

Then they turned and looked at each other for the first
time since they had come in from the garden.

Without her knowing why, her nerves began to freeze
in self-defence. He was looking at her as if she was
someone he scarcely knew. Instead of the warmth,
desire, anticipation, love even, his eyes were blank, as
empty as snow deserts.

He reached out. For a moment the warmth of his
hands on hers told her she was a fool to believe they were
separated by anything at all, then he pushed her down
in a chair and stood moodily over her without speaking,
and she knew there was this distance between them after
all.

It unrolled endlessly, endlessly, and she saw that they
were on opposite sides with the dark figure of retribution
between them and love as distant as a star.

Her eyes widened, the fullness of emotion in her heart
pressing her to tell him how she felt, how she longed for
him, how she wanted only this one thing, his love, from
him as forgiveness for the coldness they had allowed
between them.

But there was no way past the guardian who kept him
hidden behind the gates in his tower of silence. His

expression remained aloof, enigmatic, watchful, full of suspicion. It was as if he was waiting for her to walk across the wasteland between them with her heart in her hands as an offering.

It was something she could not bring herself to do, to set one foot in front of the other, to set out upon a journey whose only end might be disaster.

All she could do was wait for him, silently willing him to make the first move, to raise the portcullis a fraction, to show her that he would welcome her love, not use it against her as she feared.

Her silent plea went unheard.

Without saying anything he went over to the cabinet and fixed two drinks, returning with the Campari and soda he knew she liked. Their eyes met over the rims of their glasses as they lifted them in a silent toast. The action seemed to seal something between them, but it wasn't a mutual coming together, but rather a declaration of a continuing war. Emma began to shiver uncontrollably.

Without speaking he took the glass from between her fingers and placed it on a small table with his own. He straightened.

'Come here.' He didn't move.

Then again he put out a hand and she tried to see it as the hand of a lover, a sign that he cared. But his next words sent her illusions crashing.

'My game,' he said coolly. It took her a moment to understand what he meant. 'Well?' he went on. 'Come to me, then. What are you waiting for? It's what you want, isn't it?'

She felt herself begin to freeze.

'So?' He prompted. 'Come along.'

She couldn't move.

'Emma. It's time to collect. You thought you'd defy
me. You lost. Now you pay. It's that simple.'

'Is it?' she breathed. She succeeded in controlling her
expression so he wouldn't know what his words were
doing to her. Inside something was slowly breaking up,
grinding and tearing at her entrails, destroying her
deepest being.

'If you'll come here I'll show you how simple it is,' he
said in a harsh voice. He stood up. 'You still believe you
can fight me?' His lips twisted. Reaching down, he
gripped her by the arms and pulled her beside him. He
didn't kiss her. She was agonisingly conscious of the lips
which had recently caressed her own into a state of
submission hovering close by but now withheld. How
she longed for them. Longed to cry out for them to echo
the words of love she felt.

He put his palm against the side of her face, ungentle,
moulding her skin over the bone, withdrawing, and
pressing again so that she was swayed back and forth in
the rhythm he was creating for them. Then his other
hand started to move under her sweater. She was
powerless to respond. Transfixed by the desire to sigh
'yes' and the need to cry 'no'.

Helpless as a doll, she allowed him to drag the garment
over her head. His eyes were fixed on hers. They didn't
drop to look at her breasts, translucent beneath the black
lace camisole. Instead they stayed on hers as if he could
overpower her by the sheer force of the will that shone
from them.

A shudder ran through her as he touched the side of
her face, her neck, shoulders, the skin above her breasts,
then down in ever greater intimacy to the gleaming flesh
itself, until, making her gasp with the pang of desire, his
fingers took her nipples, teasing them to peaks of
excitement she was unable to disguise, unable to stop

her deepening breath, holding back only at the last the cry of desire that raged for release, standing instead in frozen silence, a block of ice while the fire raged within.

He bent his head with undisguised hunger, feeding his pleasure until it seemed to burn its way into her every pore. He moved over her smooth skin, dragging both hands over the bones of her back to her full hips, slithering her skirt down past her waist in one deft movement, lifting his mouth and branding her with its touch all the way to her navel, tongue licking, swirling one tiny pleasure after another into a vortex of complex sensation.

But still she would not respond. She could give no sign of the waves of exquisite pleasure his touch aroused. She would not cry out. Would not move a muscle to betray herself. It was as if he had cauterised her emotions and turned her into a being of blind sensation.

She could control her emotions when he made it plain she was only to be sacrificed to his lust to win. But she could not fight the wild sensuality his touch aroused. Her sensations could not be checked by the strength of her will even though she was able to exert such control over what she felt. It was why he could turn her into a creature of sheer animal pleasure, and why she would give no sign of it.

When her skirt lay in a pool of colour at her feet and he held her naked buttocks in the palms of his hands and pulled her yearning sex towards him, she heard the words torn from him as his head dipped and rose. 'Respond, will you? Respond to me, Emma. . .'

But she hung on to the little she had left, Tom's words in her ears. Water sign people, he had said scuttling back into your shell at the least sign of danger. You're pure emotion. But you won't trust it. You hoard it the way you hoard money and possessions. You stay in your shell and let nobody near until you've got cast-iron guarantees for your emotional safety. Learn to trust, he had told her. But now, how could she? To trust Mark del Sarto would be to trust a rattlesnake—or a scorpion.

She heard Mark insist again and again that she give in, yield to him. He ground out his demands as if he had a right to expect her to respond. She fought him. But she only had one weapon: retreat. She crept inside her shell, withdrew, let the storm rage outside where it could not harm her. It was as if her body belonged to someone else. Indeed it did. Mentally she detached herself from it. She could allow him any liberty because she was no longer there.

It would have been impossible to hand herself emotionally to a man who did not love her.

'Unfreeze——' he rasped, touching her in a way that was driving her mad with the desire to give him all he asked. But though he could do what he liked with her body, inside she was as far from being possessed as anyone could be except in the most obvious physical sense.

He knew it. He understood at once the nature of her resistance; he knew, and he resented it because it meant he was thwarted in his aim to possess her. He dragged his mouth again and again over her heated flesh, scarcely able to withdraw his lips long enough from the banquet of her body to finish what he had started to say. He seemed to lift himself with an immense effort from out of whatever deep pool of sensation he had plunged into. She felt him harden as if he had admitted aloud his determination not to be defeated by her. For a moment they wrestled in an equal contest of wills. She could feel the physical evidence of his desire against her body, heating her with pure sensation so that she almost lost control, almost lifted her arms round his neck, almost cried out to him to take her, almost begged, pleaded, as he had promised she would, almost lost the restraint that at the last moment allowed her to withdraw, to remain unmoved and unmoving in his embrace.

'What are you trying to do to me?' he demanded hoarsely. 'Are you made of ice? With no feelings? Don't you know what it is to love?'

Love, she thought. Their definitions were as different as black from white. He closed his eyes when she didn't answer, his face in anguish. 'Emma, I'm going to have you. I shall take you whether you respond to me or not. Do you think I care? I wanted it to be different, but if this is how you like it, then all right. . .'

She felt him drag her across the room and bundle her unresisting, semi-naked body through a door. She was powerless, like a doll, only her mind burning in a white heat of longing, then she felt him lower her into the darkness, spreading her limbs with his practised touch, the support of a bed covered by some silky fabric underneath her, his vibrant body against hers as he threw off his clothes, melding with her own in an assault of such excessive pleasure that she had to bite her lips to prevent the moans of ecstasy giving him the final triumph he desired.

They seemed to be matched in perfect symmetry, he in her and she taking him, her limbs flowing of their own volition over his powerful form. Through it all she clung on to her pride, allowing him nothing, no sign of a response, only at the last ecstatic moment, a rasping breath escaping her lips. He enveloped her, muscles suddenly slackening, weight bearing down on her, waves of joy and repleteness tiding through her.

She longed to cry his name, to sob out her love in the broken phrases her heart dictated, but the darker side containing the core of knowledge that told her she was merely a thing to him, to be used, and meaning less than nothing to him made her hold back the words, lock them out of reach, keeping her silent to the end.

After some moments he shifted, cradling her, caressing her silken flanks, smoothing her damp skin, lifting the hair at her nape and resting his face in the hollow of her neck. They lay together like lovers. Like lovers, she observed. It's almost as if we love each other. Mark and Emma. My Scorpio love.

There was nothing to prevent them from staying together all night. He took her again and again but, whatever pleasure he drew from her, she refused to give him the surrender he demanded. She lay silent in his arms, pleasure scouring her mind, her expression unmoved. He cursed her coldness. But she would not yield. It was tearing her in two. Her body in heaven, her soul in hell. But she could not give in.

Towards morning he carried her back to her room and placed her inside the cool sheets of her bed. 'Get some sleep. There's a lot to do tomorrow.'

He tucked her in with a gentleness that amazed her, then, before she could turn over, he went out. She slept as soundly as a child.

Next morning she was woken up by the sound of people talking in the passage outside her room. She blinked in the sunlight streaming in through the uncurtained windows, remembering how she had only reached her room in the early hours. She tried to arrange her thoughts in some sort of order as the memory of the night time enveloped her. Her body stretched under the bedclothes, a contented animal, while her mind raced with first one thought then another, judging and blaming and weighing her own behaviour and his in the light of what had taken place. She was glad she had held out, she concluded. Her body might have been his. But that was nothing to what she had held back. He would never hear her plead for him as he had arrogantly predicted, would never pirate her inner self.

As she showered and dressed she wondered with the dread of anticipation whether he would take her again as he had last night, passionately, mindlessly, lovelessly.

And, if he did, whether she would want to resist him.

The others were breakfasting in the small dining-room across the corridor when she went in. Mark was at the table with everyone else. He glanced up as she came in, then carried on with his meal. His eyes had been blank, alighting on her with scarcely a flicker of recognition.

It was like a cold shower.

She burned with the humiliation of it.

Throughout the day they failed to come face to face. She wondered if it was deliberate or merely that both of them were busy in different parts of the house. Many of the measurements had been taken by now, the various rooms, corridors and lobbies making the task a slow one, and she knew that Mark's scrupulous attention to detail demanded her utmost care. Pride would not let her turn in a slipshod piece of work.

Then night fell.

A pattern among the others seemed to have established itself already. Mark forestalled any decision she might make about going out to the village pub with them by saying he wanted to have a look at what she had done that day. She knew as soon as he turned his grey eyes on her that it was an excuse to take her to his room and make love to her.

If anything he drove her to even greater heights of sensuality, while making her even more resistant to admitting any pleasure beneath his touch. He didn't seem to care that she wouldn't beg for him as he had once demanded. It seemed enough for him to draw them both to the farthest edge of desire.

Over the weeks that followed they evolved some rules. Simple ones. Guarantees rather than rules. It came down to work during the day and loving at night, or, rather, sex at night. She knew it wasn't love. She was his sex toy.

Sometimes he would allow her to go out with the others in the evening if he himself was busy, but the rest of the time she belonged to him alone, physically, that was. Emotionally she belonged to no one but herself, and he knew it.

Twice a week he drove her back to town to see Tom and remained in the car outside the house while she went inside. Like a gaoler, she thought. I'm his prisoner. I belong to him. I'm his possession. I have no will of my own. She felt she was becoming addicted to having no will of her own. She didn't care. It didn't matter. All she dreamed of was his body taking hers, using it, doing with her whatever he wished. Nothing seemed real any more.

When she came out again he would be sitting in the driver's seat listening to the radio or making notes, or talking on the phone to one business associate or another. It was all figures, percentages, deals. He seemed to have no social contacts. Everything was money, calculation of profit and loss, though there was precious little of the latter.

Afterwards he might drive her to the restaurant where they had first dined and they would pretend they were like any other couple, except that they both knew they were acting, or they would stroll along the waterfront and he would show her how the development was taking shape. By now the offices and shopping mall were nearing completion and one phase of the residential complex was finished in its essentials, only the interiors needing work. Each apartment had its own mooring and he would take her along the private quays, showing her where the yachts would be berthed, describing where the chandlers would be, and the restaurant, and the dinghy park.

During these excursions to the outside world he treated her like any other of his employees with whom he had just a slightly more than passing interest, and it was the same during the daytime back at Larwood Hall. He was remote, untouchable, sometimes witty in an abstract sort of way, but apparently scarcely aware of the brief contact of their arms as they brushed past each other, or the accidental collision of their bodies as they entered the same door.

But at night he was another man, passionate, hungry for her, driven by insatiable desires, his dark side in control, drawing them both down into the deepest oceans of desire.

It had been the thought of this that had frightened Emma from the beginning, believing that once drawn into his realm she would drown for need of him, but she had discovered some residual strength born of fear, a sort of inner self, that seemed to be able to withstand any assault on her identity which he could impose.

It was something that drove him to further heights of passion, as if he was in the grip of a demon which could only be conquered by dragging from her the last vestiges of resistance.

But she forced herself to imagine the time when the three months were up. And how she would feel to be discarded by him. He wanted to use her up completely. To annihilate her. But she wanted to survive.

One morning, after a night of particularly exquisite

tenderness, when he had done things to her that made her want to die there in his arms, she heard him give a kind of muffled sound, his head buried in her long hair where it streamed in a dark cascade over the bed, and when she tried to lift his face so she could see what had caused him to make such a sound he resisted, digging it deeper into the pillow. Her fingers played through his hair and she tugged at the separate strands, holding them between her teeth, loving him, yes, she knew it was that, despite his desire to destroy her, but before she could come to terms with such a revelation he got up and went into the next room.

When he returned his face wore its usual bleak expression, storm-grey eyes sweeping her face with a look of utter indifference. She quailed beneath it as she always did but found the strength from inside herself not to betray by the flicker of an eyelash how her heart bled.

As he seemed about to say something she tensed, conscious of his glance inching over her naked body where she was lying voluptuously amid the confusion of pillows. Shame at being seen naked, after the things they had done together, was a thing of the past.

But he grated, 'Cover yourself up.'

Lazily raising herself on to one elbow, she looked at him in astonishment.

He came to stand by the bed. 'Why are you doing this, Emma?' He had put on a pair of jogging pants and she could see the hard outline of his sex beneath them. He still wanted her, she marvelled, even after all these weeks of loving, even after the last hours of sheer unimaginable bliss. Her own need for him was the same. Tom had been right when he had said they would be dynamite in bed. Scorpio and Cancer.

As if he had registered her thoughts about Tom he said, 'What do you and he talk about when you go back in there? How the hell does he cope knowing you're here with me? I would have thought he'd have moved out by now. He must want to break your neck.'

'Why should he?' she exclaimed.

'Why not? Have you told him you're going to go back to him?' Without waiting for an answer he said, 'Maybe you make it worth his while to stay? Maybe you keep him happy like this?' His face, she noticed, was stark with fury.

She jerked back as he lunged for her. Before she could move his hands were round her neck, fingers raking through her hair, pressuring her throat, then dragging at her chin, his lips hard on hers. He released her abruptly. 'Is he so mad for you that he'll take whatever crumbs you throw his way? Is that what you hope to drive me to, you bitch?'

'Mark! I don't understand.'

'That's always your plea,' he ground out, suddenly taking her by the shoulders and forcing her back amongst the pillows. He lay across her, pinning her beneath him, tension turning his muscles to steel as he fought to control her struggles. 'You don't understand this either?'

'What?' she managed to stutter, her head fluttering from side to side to avoid the marauding of his lips.

'This,' he breathed, bringing his mouth down over her own in a hot, pulsing movement that was strong yet gentle, seducing any reluctance she might have felt, their tongues meeting in a sudden rapture that brought tears to her eyes.

He seemed to think they were tears of pain, and when he let her go he was breathing heavily with the effort of holding himself back. His eyes ravaged her face for a moment before he said, 'I know you think you've won, but you haven't. . . not yet. . . and you never will. You can hold out and hold out, and the weeks can pass, but you can't hold out forever. I know I'll hear your cries of surrender in the end. I will have you, Emma, not only your body, but your soul, your mind, everything. And that's a promise.'

'Why, Mark? What satisfaction will it give you? Are you only interested in winning?'

'You've got it in one.'

'But why?' she cried again, struggling to sit up. He released her completely, and, brushing back her streaming hair, she reached out to grasp him by the shoulder, but he shrugged her hand away and got up without looking at her. He moved over to the window and stood for a long time gazing out into the windswept garden.

'Why?' He turned, flexing his shoulder-muscles. 'I'd have to be a psychiatrist to answer that one. Maybe it all goes back to being the youngest in a family where making it was all that counted. They were all better than me at school. Effortlessly better. Especially my elder sister.' He frowned. 'She was a brilliant linguist, mathematician——' he grimaced '—astrologer.'

He leaned against the sill. 'When she was killed I lost an ally. She'd always faked success for me. I was her pet. Her death left me exposed. I felt like a fraud—I had to prove she'd been right to favour me——' He broke off. 'Why tell you this? As if you care a damn.' He gave her a raking glance. 'But what about you?' he asked ominously. 'Let's talk about you instead.'

He moved swiftly to the bedside and sat down, putting one hand out to touch a breast, stroking it in such a way that she couldn't help melting. 'Yes,' he breathed, a little aroused himself by her immediate reaction, 'you can't get enough of me in that way, but what makes you always hold something back? What makes you delight in being such a cold, torturing, ungiving bitch?'

'If you think I torture you it must be because that's

what you want. You're the one who engineered this situation. You set it up! It's nothing to do with me. I've had no choice.'

He frowned. 'Yes, I did set it up. Deliberately. Coldly. I'll give you that much. But if I've invented the rules of the game, you've stayed to play.'

'Willingly?'

He nodded.

She gave a snort of derision.

'Yes, willingly,' he repeated. 'You could have walked out of that door at any time.'

She remembered how he had manipulated her into staying at Larwood Hall all those weeks ago. 'And been landed with a massive bill for the work you're having done in my shop?' She gave a hard laugh. 'I'd have gone out of business and you know it.'

He seemed to give a start of surprise. 'You mean that?' He raised both eyebrows. 'Really, Emma, is that it? You're staying. . .because if you didn't you would have to fork out hard cash instead?' She saw his eyes register a response that was quickly masked.

When he spoke next his voice was toneless. 'What does that make you?' The grey eyes lashed over her upturned face. 'What sort of woman does it make you, Emma?' His fingers bit into her shoulder making her wince. 'You're no better than an expensive little whore.' There was no expression on his face as he raked his fingers down her flank, then rose from the bed.

When he reached the door he turned to her. 'I'm glad we've got that straight. It's taken some time, hasn't it? At least it means I can have an easy mind about the way I've been treating you. Believe it or not, I've had a conscience about that. Now I can see how futile it was.'

He smiled and took the key from the lock. 'Stay in bed. You may as well. It's your job, isn't it? And I'll be needing you right there when I come back.' His face dead, he went out before she could move and she heard the key of the bedroom door click in the lock.

Hot rage swept over her. How *dared* he believe she was allowing this situation because of the money he was paying her? How *could* he? Yet she had invited such a verdict by the folly of her own unguarded words.

Climbing out of bed, she pulled the coverlet around her and hurried across the room. The French windows were kept locked and there was no key in evidence. She turned to the main door and rattled it, uselessly wondering if she was brazen enough to call for help and knowing she wasn't. She would die rather than be seen begging for release from a prison she had walked into of her own volition.

Raging against herself for being such a blind fool, she paced the floor, wondering what to do. When he came back, whenever that was, she would be ready for him. He couldn't keep her here if she ran out first. Then she would pack her things, get a lift to town and never return.

She curled up on the bed in the only clothes she had, a pyjama top, and nursed her anger, impatient for him to show his face.

He was wrong, wrong, wrong when he claimed she could have left Larwood Hall at any time. How could she have? There was no way to fight the lethal fascination he held for her. It had been outside her experience to deal with a man like him from the start. He had overwhelmed her. Now his lovemaking was like an addiction and she couldn't give it up.

On her first visit back home to see Tom she had confessed everything to him, hoping he would understand and could give her some advice. 'I know he doesn't care a rap about me, Tom,' she had said in a shaky voice, 'and believe me, I've really tried to fight, but I can't hold out. Something seems to be pulling us together. We're lovers now. It was inevitable from the first. It's like nothing I've ever experienced. Can you understand?'

'We two were children together,' he'd told her gently. 'I was the more experienced of the two of us, but I never aroused you to anything more than——' he'd smiled '—a level of friendly loving. I always knew you were capable of being aroused to greater heights. It was difficult to make you see that. You're such a loyal person, Emma. It blinded you to what was missing from our relationship.'

'But I feel so loving towards you, Tom, I do really.'

'But compare it to this new feeling you have for Mark.'

Slowly she had nodded. It was like comparing two different universes. 'What am I to do?' she'd whispered. 'I can't let go completely. He only wants to destroy me.'

'Does he?'

She'd nodded. 'Once I've given everything he'll throw it away. He'll throw me away. You don't know what he's like, Tom. He's not gentle and kind like you. He's driven by some dark force. It makes him utterly ruthless.'

'Don't judge him, love. You may not be getting the whole picture.'

Each week Tom had watched for signs of change. But the bleak knowledge that Mark was incapable of love showed in her expression. When Mark had asked what she and Tom talked about, she could never have told him this.

True to his word, he came back to his room after breakfast, locking the door and stripping off his shirt as he crossed to the bed.

She jerked to face him, not having expected him yet

and her plan to escape as soon as he opened the door in ruins. '*No!*' she exclaimed when she saw the expression on his face. She sprang on to her knees, her pyjama top gaping to reveal her naked breasts, but before she could drag it closed, as if that would have been any protection, he ripped it off, threw it across the floor, and dragged her hard up against him as he stood over her. He pressed her face roughly against the tight criss-cross of muscles over his stomach and she could feel the heat and the throb of his blood against her own cool skin, and then she heard the snick of a zip before both his hands scraped through her hair and cupped her head and he forced her backwards, despite her struggles, on to the bed.

'Whore,' he ground out as his pulsing body came crushing down to follow her own on to the hard mattress, 'It's time to earn your keep. We're quitting this fooling around like two adolescents in love. You're going to show me what you usually do to pay your rent.' Then his hard, dark head came down.

She struggled and fought, jerking her face from side to side in an effort to avoid the cruel pressure of his mouth over her clenched lips, but he was too strong for her and she could feel the hardness of his mouth forcing her lips apart, his probing tongue overcoming her resistance bit by bit, marauding inside her mouth with a roughness that made her gasp with pain. Swivelling her hips, she managed to thrash from side to side, hoping to free herself from the heavy weight that had her pinned beneath it, but there was no escape from beneath his raking fingers, the heavy, hot, insistent weight of him, the demon that was forcing her to give in with an urgency too powerful to withstand. He began to groan in a sort of agonised pleasure as he grew between them and then she could keep him back no longer and she heard his breathing change, rasping in and out as her humiliation reached its nadir.

In a moment it was over. He didn't speak but instead pushed her away and, feeling discarded, she rolled over on to her stomch, burying herself shame-faced into the pillow. She heard him get up and cross the room. When she lifted her head he was pulling on a pair of jeans, running his fingers rapidly through his hair at the mirror, then making for the door. He didn't even look back at her before letting himself out without a word.

She crumpled beneath the sheets, sobs racking through her whole body, till her skin was burning with the scalding of her tears.

He had left the door unlocked. She could get up and go out. She could leave now.

The thought of meeting anyone in the corridor made her recoil, but worse than that was the brokenness she felt. It was as if he had smashed her identity into little pieces.

CHAPTER TEN

BY NOW it was after two o'clock. The morning had already gone. Mark stood in the doorway. 'Are you staying here all day?' he asked.

She lay huddled on the bed, her back to him, hair covering her face. She heard him close the door and come over to the bed. He didn't touch her.

'Emma!'

When she didn't answer she felt him lift the hair concealing her eyes but she kept them shut. 'Emma,' he repeated. 'Why didn't you come down to lunch?'

She held her breath, scarcely moving.

His hand withdrew and he seemed to go away. There was silence.

She heard him cross to the door. It opened and then closed and she thought he had gone out so she turned and raised herself on one elbow. He was standing with his back to the door, watching her. She felt fiery colour flood into her cheeks.

'Pretending to be asleep?' he intoned.

She refused to answer. Instead she drew her knees up and rocked back and forth on the bed, her face buried under a veil of hair.

'Oh, Emma, please stop this. What's it for? Aren't you hungry?'

She closed her eyes and willed him to go away.

'Why are you behaving like this? For heaven's sake, get up, get dressed and come and have something to eat.'

When she didn't answer he came over to the bed again and stood there for a long time looking down at her. But he didn't touch her. Through the slit of her eyes she could see the edge of his beige trousers. He was standing beside her without moving. 'Emma?' His voice had sharpened.

When she didn't answer she saw the beige shape move away out of her line of vision.

'I'll have something sent in if you feel like staying in bed.' He went out, closing the door with a snap.

When she was alone she pulled the covers over her head. Why couldn't she get up and leave? Hot tears swirled out of her eyes, soaking her hair, making her face hot and sticky. Her lids felt raw with crying. She was past thinking about what was happening. She could only feel, and it was all anguish and emptiness. She was at the bottom of the abyss now, in the pit of hell, fires devouring her in endless agony.

She didn't hear the door open again but the sound of his voice, abrupt, uncaring, came across the room. 'I've brought it myself to save you the embarrassment of having anyone see you like this. Now get up, brush your hair and put some clothes on. You'll feel better after you've had something to eat.'

The sound of his voice was nursemaidish and it made her want to giggle, and the hysterical sound came bubbling up out of her throat, but she cut it off and it turned into a sob. She felt a hand on her shoulder.

'Come on, now, sit up.' His hands dragged, forcing her to sit. He pushed her hair back, smoothing it from off her brow, and she felt her lids flicker as she darted a glance at him. His expression was grim. She had never seen him look quite like this before. Stern. But then as always aloof too. Cold as hell. Eyes empty as the oceans.

'Where's your hairbrush?' he asked.

Waiting only for a second for the reply he obviously didn't expect, he got up and went to the bathroom, returning with his own comb and a damp sponge. He smoothed back her tangled hair, making her flinch as it caught in the snags, then wiped her face with the sponge. He got one of his shirts out of the wardrobe and made her put it on, lifting her arms as if she was a helpless child and buttoning it up to the top. 'They're right,' he observed when she was ready to his satisfaction. 'It does look better on a girl.'

Then he reached for the tray and set it on the bed beside her and began to take off the lids of the several dishes to reveal a mixture of vegetables and fish and bread. 'I didn't know what you'd want so I brought bits of everything,' he told her. He picked up a fork and put some food on it and held it to her lips.

She tightened them and turned away. 'Emma,' he remarked, 'if you don't eat I shall force you to.' He took hold of the back of her head and held it so she had to face him. 'Do you understand?'

Her eyes blazed but she couldn't speak. He had forced her down into the smallest space of all, deep within her shell, and she could go no deeper in order to escape him. The pressure of resisting forced tears into the corners of her eyes but she didn't cry. She wouldn't let him see her cry.

'Please. . .' he lowered his voice '. . . eat something. You must. It's nonsense to punish yourself by not eating. What do you gain?' He lowered the fork. For a moment he seemed defeated. Then he began to caress the back of her neck. 'Everybody's wondering where you are,' he said, turning away. 'What do you want me to tell them?'

She lowered her lashes and gazed unseeingly at the tray that separated them both. Why couldn't he release her from this horrible agony? She was being driven mad for love of him. But he would give her nothing. What did it matter what he told anyone else?

He tried the fork again. 'I mean it,' he warned. 'Eat one mouthful to show me you will and then I'll let you get on with it yourself.'

He just wanted to prove a point, show her he was stronger than she was as he'd always claimed. She opened her lips. It didn't matter. She knew she could go through the motions. Eat. Keep him quiet. What did it matter? He couldn't get at her where she was hiding. He would never winkle her out, crush her, destroy her. She was too strong inside where it mattered.

She took a morsel of food and chewed it without looking at him. He seemed satisfied by this and handed her the fork. She felt like stabbing him with it. She could have gouged his eyes with one blow. But what did it matter? She picked at the food on one of the plates. Eating rapidly, finding it difficult to swallow at first because of the lump in her throat, but forcing it down, half-chewed, getting rid of it so he would have no reason to go on forcing her against her will.

'Good,' he said when she finished. He picked up the tray and went to the door. 'Are there any clothes you want me to fetch from your room?' He waited for an answer but when it was obviously not forthcoming he went out.

She curled up on the bed again. She would go soon. Or would she? She didn't care now where she was, it was all one. Hell was everywhere. She was walking through flames.

Time seemed to have no scale and she didn't know whether he had left her for a minute or an hour but he was back, tossing a heap of clothes to her. 'Get dressed,' he ordered.

When she didn't move he came closer. There was a sigh of impatience in his voice. 'If you don't, I suppose I

shall have to do it for you. Now come on.' When he bent
down and started to try to pull a sweater over her head
she squirmed away from him and picked up the collec-
tion of garments herself, slipping into panties, tights and
skirt in a trice. When she pulled on the skirt she had to
stand up and he moved next to her as if to prevent her
from sinking back on to the bed again. 'That's better.
Now come on.'

He marched her towards the door. She noticed he had
one of her coats over his arm. 'Where are we going?' she
blurted, suddenly digging in her heels.

'Good. You've got your voice back.' He pushed her
out into the corridor.

'No!' She struggled to get out of his grip but he
tightened it, putting one hand firmly around her waist
and forcing her towards the outer door. Unwillingly but
too defeated to put up a fight, she allowed him to propel
her across the gravel to his car, and when he opened the
passenger door and guided her inside she gave in like a
rag doll.

He locked her door from outside then got in beside
her. Without explanation he started the engine and began
to drive towards the gates.

Emma closed her eyes. It was a matter of supreme
indifference to her where they went. She assumed he
had grown tired of her and was now going to dump her
back in town. Let him. She was glad. It was what she
wanted. She had had enough. He might think he had
won. But he hadn't. She would survive.

When she opened her eyes they were gliding to a stop
outside her shop. It was the first time she had seen it
since leaving it nearly two months ago. Now she was
surprised at the transformation. Bereft of all the familiar
pretty things, its façade was obliterated by scaffolding
and builders ladders were everywhere.

He let her out of the car and guided her through the open door into a chaos of dust and rubble. Workmen were busy and the sound of hammering made speech impossible, but she saw that the whole place was being restored to its former style, ceiling decorations being remoulded, cornices put in where once they were missing, window-frames restored to the original pattern.

He led her to the back and she got a shock to find that the old door had been removed, an old archway revealed and beyond that a cobbled arcade with a water-pump and partly restored drinking-fountain. It was almost back to the way it had been before the ravages of the twentieth century had laid everything to waste.

It was going to be beautiful when it was finished. She didn't know what to say. What did he expect her to say? She gazed around without speaking. The work was being done so thoroughly, she knew it far exceeded the few repairs he had asked her to do. She was puzzled when she turned to him.

'When did you plan this?' she asked.

'After that public meeting when you were so impassioned about the place. I didn't realise what I'd bought. It had looked like nothing on the surface. Then I came in and had a really good look round.'

'Don't you need planning permission to do all this?'

'We're only revealing what was already there, and I don't imagine the planning department are likely to refuse me anything. I plan to develop the whole area with this courtyard as its focal point. There's a path at the back, a right of way leading down to the quays. It should revitalise a very neglected side of town.' He pointed to the buildings in the arcades. 'They'll be turned into shops,' he told her. 'The sort that will enhance the sort of things you sell. Soft furnishings. A picture framers. An art gallery.' He turned to her.

'Mark. . .' She bit her lip. 'I don't know what to say.'
A memory of what he had forced her to do that morning
flooded over her. She turned her head and began to walk
off rapidly towards the sanctuary of what had once been
her own little shop: It was a shell now, but she went
inside, crossing into what had been her office, her inner
sanctum.

He followed her, but stopped on the threshold. 'I've
got something to do. Will you stay here and wait for me?
I won't be long.'

Without waiting for an answer he went out.

In his absence she had a good look round. There was
a new wooden stair-rail up to the upper floor. Previously
the stairs had been too shaky to be used and the floor
above had gaped with missing floorboards, making it too
dangerous to use. Now she saw she could keep some of
her stock upstairs, perhaps bedroom furniture, beautiful
old-fashioned beds, things like that. . . She stopped.
What was she thinking? She would never be able to
afford to carry on trading here. The leasehold would be
astronomical. Why on earth had he shown it to her? To
taunt her with what she had lost?

She went outside. Maybe he had won after all. What
did she have left? Nothing, it seemed. Not even her
pride, not after this morning. She went to sit on the edge
of the drinking-trough and it was here he found her.

She saw him come out of the shell of the shop and
come to a halt beneath the arcade. Something had
happened. One look at his face was enough.

'Mark? What's the matter?' She got up and hurried
over before she realised what she was doing. She stopped
abruptly halfway across the courtyard. He seemed to
move towards her like a man in a dream with such a look
of—what was it?—that she felt her breath contract.
'Mark?'

He stopped a few yards in front of her, eyes never leaving her face. He said simply, 'You'd better go home.'

'What?' She moved towards him. 'What for?' A hand came to her mouth. Tom! It must be Tom, something had happened. But how did Mark know that?

The answer came almost at once. 'I've just been along to your house. . .' He turned suddenly and began to walk off.

'Mark!' she called, abruptly coming to life. 'Wait! What's happened?' But although he must have heard her he didn't pause and by the time she had raced after him through the shop he was already climbing into his car. By the time she got to the door he was tearing off up the road.

Tom, oh, my dear, she thought frantically, setting off at a run along the pavement. Mark must have driven off like that to fetch a doctor. Guilt and panic mingled as she covered the distance to the house, sending her running two at a time up the steps to go bursting in through the open front door.

When she skidded to a halt in the living-room her eyes opened in astonishment. 'Tom!' she exclaimed.

He was sitting in his usual place by the fire with the familiar plaid rug around his knees, the same gentle smile, the same burnished blond hair, the same patient, calm, understanding, but above all living man she had known so long.

'Oh, God, I thought you were dead!' She collapsed against him, wrapping her arms tightly round his neck. 'Oh, Tom, my dear angel, I thought you were lying on the floor all helpless—I thought—oh, I don't know what I thought. My dear love, thank heavens I was wrong!'

'You silly child, what made you think a thing like that?' Then he smiled. 'He came to see me.' There was no need to name him.

She sank down on to the rug and buried her face in his lap. Then the sobs shook through her in a storm of release, racking her whole frame until eventually there was nothing left inside. It was then Tom stopped stroking her hair and said, 'Hadn't you two better have a good talk?'

'I can't. He hates me, Tom. He just wanted me to use as some——' a sob strangled the next words but she forced it out '——some sex object, without any feeling. He just wanted me to give in to him so he could know he'd won. But I can't help feeling. . .wanting him—I love him so much, it's like being in hell.'

'What a couple of fools. This is the trouble with Scropio and Cancer, they both want cast-iron guarantees before they risk themselves. What havoc it can cause.'

'How did you know he was Scorpio?' she asked through her tears.

He laughed. 'What else? All that high-powered energy, forever the dynamic businessman, the self-control, the apparent hardness. And underneath. . .real passion, deep feelings, fidelity.' He laughed softly. 'And you'd never guess to look at him.'

'He's hateful. A monster. There's nothing underneath.'

'Well, actually,' began Tom, 'there is this other side, Emma. You'll see it if you take a good look——'

'You'd justify Attila the Hun if you had to,' she tried to joke, dabbing at her eyes. 'Anyway, he's gone. He's just driven off like a madman. Which proves my point. And now I'm here. I'm back. I'm safe with you again. And I'm never ever going back to Larwood Hall.'

There was a cheery call from outside and at that moment Angelika came in loaded down with shopping bags. 'The front door was open——' she said, then stopped. 'Emma! Lovely to see you. Are you staying to tea?'

Emma rose hurriedly to her feet. But before she could move Tom reached out and took her by the hand. 'Where are you going?'

'She's not going anywhere, I hope,' exclaimed Angelika coming right into the room. 'I'll just pop these things away then put the kettle on. Won't be a tick.'

After she'd gone Emma looked down at Tom. 'I'm sorry. I'd momentarily forgotten you were both getting on so well. I'll only be in the way.' A sob blocked her throat for a moment, a double sense of loss so overwhelming that she could scarcely fight it off.

'Foolish creature. How can you be in the way? You live here.' Tom held on to her hand. 'Do you think I'd throw you into the street? You'd never be in the way. And don't forget it's half your house too. You're the one who's been keeping up the payments.'

'How mercenary, but actually I don't mind about that,' she said as lightly as she could. 'I know Cancerians are supposed to put money and nest-eggs and all that sort of thing above everything else but I really think we're square. After all, you helped me start the antique business. I've still got the stock.'

'I'm being clumsy. What I mean is, you don't have to go away if you don't want to. I shouldn't even have to tell you that,' he reproved. 'But at the same time, you must sort out this matter with Mark.'

For the first time she wondered what the two men had had to say to each other. 'At least he didn't punch you in the jaw as he once threatened,' she said. 'But what did he say to you?'

'He doesn't give much away, but he looked pretty damn shocked to find the man he'd been thinking of as a rival all this time was nothing but a cripple.'

'Tom! Stop it!'

'It's true!' Tom was grinning. 'He came storming in
as if he was going to tear the place apart with his bare
hands. But I kind of took the wind out of his sails!' He
looked very pleased with himself.

Emma crouched down in front of him. 'Why do you
say he thought of you as a rival?'

'Why don't you ask him yourself?'

Her head dropped. 'How? Nothing will make me give
him the satisfaction of chasing after him. That's what
he's always wanted. Longing for me to beg and plead.
Well, I won't. Let him go. I'm not going to chase him.'

Over the next day the three of them established a routine
that was cosy on the surface at least, if not, from Emma's
point of view, so cosy beneath. She felt like a hollow
ghost, keeping up a front for Tom and Angelika, all the
while knowing that Tom for one wasn't fooled.

She had her hands in a bowl of washing-up water on
the second morning when there was a ring at the door.
Angelika was doing something for Tom in the sitting-
room so she went to answer it expecting the postman or
window-cleaner or someone like that.

It was Mark.

'Hi!' He stood on the threshold for a moment, simply
staring in at her. Then before she could move he was
thrusting himself inside, sending her backing away to
avoid the contagion of his touch. She knew if he once
laid a finger on her she would cave in.

'I drove off like that because there was simply too
much to accept. I couldn't face you. Now I can. I've had
time to think.'

She said nothing. What was there to say? So he had
done some thinking. No doubt he would want to tell her
that of course the contract was terminated as from that

terrible morning when he had demonstrated the contempt in which he held her.

'You'd better come into the kitchen,' she told him in a stiff voice. 'Angelika and Tom are in the sitting-room.' She led the way, walking rapidly with head erect in front of him, hurrying because he seemed to be almost trampling on her heels. When they were inside he closed the door as if shutting off any chance of escape.

'Right. So what's it all about?' he began.

'I'm sorry,' she replied in a prim voice, feeling rather proud of her self-control, 'I don't understand.' Then she bit her lip. This was his accusation before. But it was true. She didn't. Nobody should have this effect on anybody else. She didn't know how it was possible. She was ashamed of it. But she couldn't explain all that. He would only crow to learn that she had been driven so crazy for him. After all, that was what he had always wanted.

'Answer me one question. Have you ever understood the power you've had over me?' Before she could make sense of what he was saying he went on, 'Meeting you changed me. Up till then I'd lived and breathed work. There was nothing else. I wanted nothing else. Women came and went. They were just passing through, not even ruffling the surface. But then you came along. You went straight to my heart.' He gave a grimace. 'Have I got a heart? Maybe not after the way I've treated you.'

His lips twisted. 'I should have understood you better, especially after seeing you get up on that platform that first time I ever set eyes on you and make your speech. I could tell you were nervous, that you'd never done anything like that before. But you were so impassioned, you forgot your fear. At the end of it everybody there, including me, was on your side.'

He took two strides across the kitchen and came to a

stop in front of her. 'Emma, why did you let me treat you the way I did? Why didn't you stop me? Couldn't you see that once I'd started I couldn't turn back? I didn't want it to be like that.' His face was grey. He put out one hand. 'Oh, my love,' he said, 'it was the last thing in my mind to hurt you. . . I thought you were soft and vulnerable but when I came close you seemed to close up against me. I began to think you were incapable of hurt. I made myself believe you were like stone all the way through.'

She was transfixed by the agonised expression on his face. Was this Mark del Sarto? The man of iron who had driven her close to the brink of despair?

He took her silence for hostility. 'I know it's no good. There's no reason why you should ever want to see me again. But I couldn't leave things as they were. A clean break is best.' He said, 'I dared not risk telling you how I felt before now. I didn't want to be hurt. If you'd known how I felt I would have been totally in your power. And if you'd left me, you would have taken my whole world with you.'

He moved away and began to stalk around the kitchen as if preparing his thoughts in a way that would make sense to her. 'I felt that by loving you when you seemed to love someone else I was being dragged down beneath the surface into some monstrous and dangerous region where I could easily go mad. I was being sucked down among shoals of madness, Emma, can you see that? It was as if something was drawing me on. I couldn't pull back.'

His words reminded her of how she had felt, the addiction of his touch drawing her on in a way she couldn't resist.

When she remained silent he went on, 'I tried to give you time—that night at my club taught me how I was rushing things when you slapped me down so decisively. I tried to pull back a little to give you chance to discover me for yourself, time to get over your terrible defensiveness. Don't forget, I knew what to expect from your birth sign—and it warned me to tread gently. That was the difficult part, because I simply wanted to possess you totally and at once.'

'Like a robber baron,' she breathed. 'Yes.'

His eyes were like slate. 'I was crazy with jealousy over this mysterious man in the background. But at first I didn't doubt I could prise you away from him. . . and that was my intention. I had no qualms about what I was doing. I wanted to smash him out of existence. I guess I really need your gentleness and sensitivity, Emma, just as you maybe need my——' He paused looking uncertain of himself for once. 'As it turns out, I think we both need each other,' he went on. 'We have different things we can give each other.' He shrugged the broad shoulders. There was a hint of apology in the movement and his face was touched with regret. 'It was a hell of a shock when I met Tom at last. He's a terrific guy and I understood at once why you couldn't leave him, even though he tells me he's with someone else these days.' He looked uncomfortable and went on, 'If I say I was crazy about you've got to believe it—you seem to possess the power to drive me over the edge of reason.' He turned bleak eyes on hers. 'There, I've said it all. You have the power to destroy me. Use it. After what I've done to you I deserve nothing less.'

Emma gripped the side of the table against which she had been pressing for support. 'Is this true?' she breathed. 'Do you really feel something. . .?'

'Emma, with one gesture you transformed my dead existence into living colour.' He stepped closer, his cloud grey eyes on her face, his voice roughening. 'You gave life a meaning that has nothing to do with success, or money or the price of things. When you told me you were only staying at Larwood Hall because I was paying you—it put me in hell. It had meant so much to live with you like husband and wife, sharing our days, our nights, taking you into my bed night after night, even though all the time I knew I had never quite captured your secret self. I made myself wait until you really trusted me enough to say what I wanted to hear. I wanted to hear those words of need that echoed how I felt about you. I had to be an optimist, otherwise I would never have been able to go on like that—night after night, going silently through the motions of love, not knowing whether you cared a damn for me or not.'

Emma watched Mark still struggling to put his feelings into words and now all she longed to do was tell him what was in her own heart. 'At first I tried to keep you at arm's length because it seemed as if you wanted to destroy me, my shop, my life. I tried to appear indifferent to you,' she admitted in a rush. She gave him a scared glance. 'Anything rather than admit how much I needed you, wanted you.'

She saw him give a start.

'Later,' she hurried on before her courage failed, 'I primed myself again and again to say something, just a word, a little word, to tell you how much you meant so that I could have scurried to safety if you'd rejected me. I kept thinking you were only interested in getting the tenants out of your building. And you wouldn't give me a chance to say anything to bring us closer. You were so masked, so shut off. I couldn't tell what you felt or what you thought and I dared not risk letting you know how I felt.'

With a sudden smile she said, 'It was like approaching

a scorpion. You were already inside your shell, the barb ready to strike me dead if I approached. . .'

'Is this true? You care? Even now after what I've put you through?'

She nodded, blinking the tears out of her eyes. Did she love him? Was he mad? She lived and breathed for him.

'We've allowed an ocean of misunderstanding to come between us—all because we haven't dared to risk our hearts,' he murmured.

'Cast-iron guarantees. Nothing less will do for either Scorpio or Cancer folk.' She smiled. It seemed like the first time in weeks.

Mark's face was beginning to express all the love he had bottled up for so long. He was illumined by it, nothing held back. His eyes flashed silver and bright.

In one flash of movement he was across the kitchen and they were locked in each other's arms. 'I love you, love you. . .' he murmured over and over again, holding her tightly against him, measuring her beating heart against his own. They were together at last. Home and safe.

By the time the refurbishment of Larwood Hall was completed it was midsummer. The sun had moved through the houses of heaven until it stood in the sign of the crab.

Everything had gone well; the planning authorities gave the go-ahead to Mark's building restoration scheme in town and, now that there was no opposition, the work proceeded without a hitch.

Emma opened her newly designed shop as part of her birthday celebrations at the beginning of July and afterwards they held a special reception at Larwood Hall to which Angelika was able to bring Tom. When all the official well-wishers had departed the four of them sat in the conservatory and talked things over. Mark had a proposal to make, he told them.

'In fact,' he said with one of those unexpected smiles which had turned Emma's heart over from the very first, 'I have two proposals. One concerns you and Angelika,' he said to Tom. 'It's to do with the annexe. Simply, it needs someone to live in it, so what do you think?' He glanced from one to the other.

Later, when they'd gone off to inspect their new home, Angelika pushing Tom's wheelchair down the ramp that had already been installed, Mark turned to Emma. 'I know you're good at arithmetic. Aren't you going to ask me what the second proposal is?' He took her by the hand. 'Or have you already guessed?'

She lifted eyes brimming with love to his. 'Spell it out for me so there can be no misunderstandings.'

'All those are in the past,' he told her, 'at least, if you say yes they will be. Will you, Emma? Will you marry me?'

She closed her eyes as he lifted her fingers and pressed them to his lips one by one with a gesture as gentle as any she could desire. He told her, 'It's taken me a long time to risk telling you how much I love you. But I'm yours now, Emma, for as long as you care to have me.'

'That's going to be forever, my love,' she replied in a soft voice, and then she spoke the words he had wanted to hear all along. 'I love you, Mark. I want you, I need you and I long for you every minute of my life.'

And it was true, for she knew her surrender was as complete as his own. Their love was out in the open, there was nothing to fear, and it had the sort of all-time guarantee that any Scorpio man and Cancer woman could ever desire.

STARGAZING

YOUR STAR SIGN: **CANCER (June 22–July 23)**

CANCER is the first of the Water signs, ruled by the Moon and controlled by the element of Earth. These combinations tend to make you extremely sensitive even though you may appear tough and protected by your crab-like shell! While you are generous and kind, others should be wary as you always expect something in return!

Socially, you tend to prefer several close relationships and you love taking care of things and people. At home you can be loving, indulgent and forgiving most of the time but friends should beware—you hate any sort of intrusion or disruption in your life.

Your characteristics in love: Cancerians are the great romantics—highly emotional and soft-hearted, you are not one for light-hearted flirtations! But partners should beware—you are often afraid of being hurt and your natural defence mechanism means loved ones must always be careful about what they say! None the less, your natural affection and loyalty means that people are attracted to you—you are never likely to be short of romance in your life!

Star signs which are compatible with you: Scorpio, Pisces, Taurus and **Virgo** are the most harmonious, while you may well have met your match if you choose **Capricorn**, **Aries** or **Libra** as your partner! Other signs can also be compatible, depending on which planets reside in their Houses of Personality and Romance.

What is your star-career? Cancerians love to take care of people or animals and have a natural potential to be good nurses, doctors, social workers, teachers and therapists—in fact, any job which involves looking after others! Positions which involve talking to people will also appeal to you—child care, personal management, banking or writing will bring out your natural ability for communication.

Your colours and birthstones: As your sign is ruled by the Moon, there is little surprise in knowing that your birthstones are moonstone and pearl, whose milky hues both indicate the Moon's influence over your life. The ocean pearl was once regarded by ancient astrologers as a symbol of chastity and purity but was also thought to encourage greed!

Cancerians, with their influences of the Earth and Moon, tend to go for pale colours which you will find have a calming and soothing influence over your life!

CANCER ASTRO-FACTFILE

Day of the week: Monday
Countries: New Zealand and Holland
Flowers: Marigolds, water-lily and wild flowers
Food: Pears, white fish; Cancerians make wonderful cooks and are excellent home-makers. They enjoy preparing food such as creamy dishes for others but do themselves have a tendency to overeat!
Health: Be careful not to let upsets get the better of you or you will be plagued with digestive problems! The ribs, sternum and digestive organs are often sensitive so beware of heartburn and gastric disorders which can happen when someone upsets a Cancerian's sensitive nature. Lots of friends, sensible eating and emotional happiness are the key to your overall well-being.

You share your star sign with these famous names:

The Princess of Wales

Esther Rantzen

Meryl Streep

Daley Thompson

Tom Cruise

Ringo Starr

Harrison Ford

Wayne Sleep

ZODIAC LOVE MATCH

CALL THE MILLS & BOON
LOVE MATCH HOTLINE

The only service to give you a detailed love analysis of your own star sign and then tell you how romantically compatible you are with the man of your dreams.

If you're interested in hearing how you match up with that special man in your life, or just want to know who would suit you best, all you have to know is your own star sign and that of the man you're interested in hearing yourself matched with.

If you dial the special Love Match 'phone number shown below, we will connect you to Catriona Roberts Wright who will give you an in-depth report on how compatible your two signs are.

CAN YOU BEAR TO WAIT?

DIAL 0898 600 077 NOW

Relax in the sun with our Summer Reading Selection

Four new Romances by favourite authors, Anne Beaumont, Sandra Marton, Susan Napier and Yvonne Whittal, have been specially chosen by Mills & Boon to help you escape from it all this Summer.

Price: £5.80. Published: July 1991

Available from Boots, Martins, John Menzies, W.H. Smith, Woolworths and other paperback stockists.

Also available from Mills and Boon Reader Service, P.O. Box 236, Thornton Road, Croydon, Surrey CR9 3RU.

Next month's Romances

Each month, you can choose from a world of variety in romance with Mills & Boon. These are the new titles to look out for next month.

SOME KIND OF MADNESS Robyn Donald

A FORBIDDEN LOVING Penny Jordan

ROMANCE OF A LIFETIME Carole Mortimer

THE MOST MARVELLOUS SUMMER Betty Neels

TATTERED LOVING Angela Wells

GYPSY IN THE NIGHT Sophie Weston

PINK CHAMPAGNE Anne Weale

NIGHTS OF DESIRE Natalie Fox

DARK GUARDIAN Rebecca King

YOURS AND MINE Debbie Macomber

FROM THE HIGHEST MOUNTAIN Jeanne Allan

A FAIR EXCHANGE Valerie Parv

AFTER THE ROSES Kay Gregory

SPRING SUNSHINE Sally Cook

DANGEROUS ENGAGEMENT Lynn Jacobs

ISLAND MASQUERADE Sally Wentworth

STARSIGN

THE TRAGANA FLAME Jessica Marchant

Available from Boots, Martins, John Menzies, W.H. Smith, Woolworths and other paperback stockists.

Also available from Mills and Boon Reader Service, P.O. Box 236, Thornton Road, Croydon, Surrey CR9 3RU.